PHENGARIS

ANNA ORRIDGE

First Published in Great Britain in 2025 by Nefarious Bat Press

Cover art and design by Ruth Anna Evans

Editing by TC Parker

For Gareth, who did not mind being the inspiration for an eldritch horror

PROLOGUE

Who knew humans could be so colourful inside? Especially one as dull as Rob had been, when he was alive.

The perfectly round gouge in his belly still had its sharp rim. There remained a purple slash of liver, the yellow of the pancreas visible even under congealed blood. And the gall bladder had the same wet, dark green look as a vine leaf wrap.

He was lying on his back. The blood had pooled, creating a livid spirit level along the back of his calves. A long horizon of bruise.

Although she was kneeling right beside the corpse, Aurora didn't gag at the stench. Her sense of smell wasn't the same as it had been even a week ago. She could still identify the faecal-sweet smell as flesh rot, but it no longer triggered her disgust.

It was right Rob had died here in the insect house, amongst his bugs. Most of the poor critters would probably join him in death in a week or so, since his body had already been lying undiscovered for three days. Nobody had cared or even been curious enough to look for the poor bastard yet.

He'd been complaining of abdominal pain for some weeks before the final confrontation. She'd told him it was constipation and given him some of her herbal remedies – which were, in fact, sedatives. She upped the dose, but not so quickly that he'd notice his increasing sleepiness.

But then he had noticed something – the swelling in the area beneath his diaphragm – and decided to go to the doctor. Of course, Aurora couldn't let him get anywhere near a hospital.

She'd meant to do it with a swift slash to the neck from behind, while he was opening the tank to feed some of his beetles. But he'd turned around at just the wrong time and seen the blade in her hand, resulting in exactly the sort of panic she'd hoped to avoid. In the aftermath, she was too busy thinking about how to get rid of her bloodied clothes to worry about the open tank.

The beetles that had escaped had not gone hungry, at any rate.

She could see at least three of them now, in the gouged-out wound of his exposed belly. They were large with distinctive, wavering stripes on their carapaces – the black and the amber of traffic lights. At a fleeting glimpse, you could take them for bees. They were attractive little things, really. She wished she had a magnifying glass to see their little mouth parts do their tearing and ripping.

She had a quick look at his face as she got to her feet. All the emotion had sagged away in the later stages of livor mortis; the jaw hanging open slightly, eyes closed.

But what remained of his spirit still had that anger and fear that might well have ended in her own murder. She knew this, because she was cradling that remnant in her arms.

It was about the same size as a newborn baby. She'd cut off its wings yesterday to prevent it flying away, then swaddled it. But as she touched its chitinous head with her lips, Rob's inchoate rage quivered through her mind like ripples from a stone.

ONE

Some people can get high anywhere. But Mark required the kind of ambience which only Thurstrop Wood could provide.

He had to walk up a few steeply uphill streets to get there. Since it was January, most people hadn't taken their Christmas decorations down yet: the neatly trimmed suburban hedges were still draped with necklaces of winking lights.

A little unmarked alley between houses switched abruptly from plywood fences to a nettle-strewn pathway. Excitement, mingled with the comfort of familiarity, seeped through him as he walked down it.

Usually, he just found a felled tree to sit on, his smoking accompanied by the brief blasts of a woodpecker somewhere overhead. Tonight, however, he couldn't relax.

He'd been caught by cops twice last year. One more possession charge and he'd have his sorry arse hauled in front of the magistrate, Constable Parks had assured him. No more Cautions And Quiet Words With Mum shit for him.

The thought of that made him grin. Parks couldn't have spoken to his mother even if he'd wanted to. She could barely croak out a sentence. Pretty soon she wouldn't be taking any more rancid, rum-soaked breaths, either.

Mark didn't want to think about his mother or her illness or the stench of urine and disinfectant that now filled the house in place of the sickly fruity aroma that trailed her during her years of alcoholism; it was the olfactory equivalent of the tang that lingered in the back of the throat after you'd been sick. No wonder he preferred drugs to booze.

All he wanted tonight was to savour the last bit of his weed and try the new pills he'd got from Simp.

And if there was one place he was pretty much certain to avoid police officers, or anybody else for that matter – it was the scrapyard between the wood and Thurstrop Lane.

Most people in town steered well clear of the wood. His mother had always warned him off it. And he realised as he got older that it was because it had a reputation as a cruising spot. That was the initial draw for him, in fact, along with the chance to smoke in peace. But he'd never come across any other guys looking for a good time. Just the odd dog walker.

The scrapyard was something different, though. It wasn't even like one of those abandoned old houses, with kids daring each other to ring on the doorbells and everyone claiming they'd seen creepy figures in the window. Derelict places normally gather stories – especially in crappy little dormitory suburbs like this one, where everyone was bored shitless. But when it came to the old yard, there was just a queasy silence.

Mark didn't believe in supernatural shit. He'd had to sit next to Mum too many times in the early stages of her illness, watching daytime TV psychics flatter credulous pensioners. The yard *was* weird, though, and he had always steered clear of it before. How come some developer hadn't taken it over and built a fake Tudor McMansion, like the ones on the other side of the wall?

Most of the fence that enclosed the yard was covered with encroaching foliage. Over it, there wasn't much to see. Two old sheds had collapsed, their rotting timbers protruding skywards. The brambles climbing up the walls of the sheds were like string tied taut around a pig carcass.

Fuck it, though. It was perfect for getting stoned without unwelcome interruptions.

Mark got out his mobile and switched on the torch function. He didn't have to sweep the light across the wire fence too many times before he found a nice, wide gap at the bottom, almost like the entrance to a tent. He crawled through it easily, only getting a few scratches from the brambles.

Once he was in the yard itself, he let out a whistle. This was *not* what he'd been expecting.

The yard was full of rusting metal. But they weren't old cars or washing machines. They were works of art – gigantic insect sculptures crafted out of scrap metal, and all sorts of other rubbish. A beetle with metallic helmets for wings raised its TV aerial antennae to the sky. Elsewhere, an enormous ant, its thorax and abdomen crafted from what looked like repurposed old globes, still with strips of faded paper attached. A fly with cracked Perspex wings perched on a rotten log.

The moonlight gave the whole place a strange shimmer.

Looking back down, he gasped and swore. "Who the fuck are you?"

A dark silhouette stood in front of him, four or five metres away.

He blinked. Fear ran a tight, rapid arpeggio down the back of his neck. It was too dark to make out a face, but he could see weirdly long legs in... combat shorts?

Then the reality of it hit him, and he stumbled backwards, laughing, before remembering he needed to keep quiet here. Parks and all.

It was a mirror. A fucking mirror. Christ, he wasn't even stoned yet.

He staggered in closer, to get a proper look. It was big, circular, propped up against the wire fence. Some kind of metal thing stuck out of its centre – a dagger, maybe?

Squinting, he saw the mirrored surface had Roman numerals delicately etched into it, and that the dagger was actually a pointer – a sundial, no less. An absolutely huge one too, almost his height. The ones he'd seen before had generally been the size of plates, in people's gardens alongside the bird baths. But he did remember once seeing one stuck to the side of some heritage building Mum had taken him to visit, and this was quite similar. Like a huge shield.

Wedged into the triangular gap between the pointer and the surface of the sundial was a delicate cast iron tracery of a grasshopper.

He got up and patted the top of the thing. It was weird how clean the surface seemed, free of smears or scratches. Quite a nice bit of metal, actually: the kind his dad would once have taken back from a building site to keep in the workshop. Odd for it to have been abandoned like this. You could probably sell it for a fair amount on one of those online auction sites.

Anyway, this was turning into one fuck of a night. He was supposed to be unwinding.

A little music would sort him out, he thought. He found

a large log near one of the sheds and sat down. The moss felt cool and velvety against his legs.

Getting out his earbuds, he put his phone on random play, then poured a few of Simp's pills from the envelope into his palm. They were shaped like little coral pink shells. Kind of cute, actually – like sweets in a kiddie's party bag.

They weren't meant for him, of course. They were for his mother.

Mum had been on morphine for a while now. It came in liquid form, and Mark had to squirt it into her mouth. It had helped kill the pain and get her to sleep for a long time, but now it wasn't strong enough.

Neither her pain nor her tiredness elicited much sympathy from him in the early stages. It wasn't like she was in the habit of making a fuss over him when he was sick, after all. She'd been the sort of parent who'd gleefully push him out of the door to school, even when he had snot running down his face and his throat was raw.

But Mark had learned that once pain reaches a certain level, crosses a certain threshold, it becomes like a yowling, demanding pet; a separate being, almost, from the person suffering it.

For a while, Mum's eyes had followed him round the room. When she could, she'd gasp out for help – and pain like that extracts sympathy and action, whatever your underlying feelings. He didn't feel any urge to tend to his mother, but he certainly had to tend to *that*.

After a few sleepless nights listening to her groaning and muffled sobs, he'd gone to see Simp. "Do you know something that'll knock someone out reliably?" he'd asked. "But without killing them?"

Simp came back to him with a wink and a sachet full of the pink shells. "No more than one every three hours. And mind she doesn't take too much water with it. Sleep's guaranteed, but the hallucinations are pretty wild, so you'll need to watch her."

Mark was surprised Mum hadn't resisted or asked him any questions when he presented her with this mysterious new medicine that quite obviously hadn't come from a pharmacy. She'd never liked pills when she was healthy, not even paracetamol.

But she stared down at the little pink shells in her palm, then swallowed them dry, her yellowing throat undulating.

After that, just as Simp had promised, there was sleep. Unbroken sleep, with no buzzing for the commode at 3am in the morning. Bliss.

He tipped back his head, swallowed two of the pills dry and let his thoughts turn back to music.

The first song to come on was one of his own remixes. He'd taken the opening chords from one of his favourite dungeon synth tracks, then had the guitars disintegrate in the face of a relentless drill beat. He couldn't help but chuckle softly – wasn't this just what he needed, to soothe his nerves?

As the singer's bellow joined the rasp of the saw synthfo, he lay back on the log and rolled a joint. He stuck it between his teeth and took the lighter out of his pocket. It sparked a few times, but no joy. When the flame finally came, it bounced up and down in the wind like a ball captured in stop motion.

The light flickered against the metal carapace of the huge beetle nearby. But most of the yard was now cast in shadows.

He lit up and lifted the joint to his lips, letting the sweet, earthy smoke tickled his nostrils. He inhaled quickly and breathed the smoke out to the stars.

Above the music, he heard a bird call. He didn't recognise it, but the rhythm was quite distinct.

Dad had been a birder. He used to have all these funny little mnemonics, like Cockney rhyming slang, to remember each individual bird song. It didn't work for the nuthatch, though, with its noisy ululation – the aural equivalent of a merry-go-round pole.

This one was quite catchy. Mark had a go at making up some words for it, the way he sometimes would with one of his electronic tracks.

Little bit of hash, a hand job and some POOOOOOOOOO-PPERS...

A raucous croak from behind startled him. He turned round, blinking in the darkness.

There was a large chestnut tree in the corner of the scrapyard and, beneath its canopy, a series of mounds. It was, maybe, an abandoned badger sett. But it was huge – at least three feet high.

At first, he thought what he saw in front of it was a piece of rubbish, tossed about by the wind. Only the thing was round. He wondered for a moment it might be a desiccated Christmas wreath, blown off someone's house.

He approached it cautiously. Turning off the music on his phone, he switched on the torch function and pointed it at the ground.

With a brief shock, he realised he was looking at a jay – no mistaking that splash of peach. It was in some kind of trap – a sphere made of very fine wire mesh?

Dad had always been in favour of putting a creature out of its misery. Mark had seen him do it a few times on the road. He'd never been distressed by the sight of it; only in awe of Dad's strong hands as he wrapped his fingers round the neck. But he wasn't sure he could do it himself.

He walked over to the bird. It was making a series of low rattles, clicks and rusty gate noises. Dad, who shared Mark's taste in music, had once called jays nature's scratch DJs.

He crouched and touched the sphere. Instantly, it disintegrated – collapsing like a house of cards. Mark yelped and snatched his hand back, dropping his mobile in the process. The dropped phone illuminated the ground in front of him. Spiders? No, those were *ants*. Fucking huge ones, almost the size of daddy-long-legs, and with strange green dots on their bodies. He felt a surge of revulsion.

What in holy fuck was the jay doing in the middle of them like that? Had they... *ambushed* it?

Once they'd all disappeared into the crevices of the log, draining away like water down a plug, Mark's breathing slowed. He made his way slowly to the jay.

It flapped its wings at his approach, squawking and flying at him. He instinctively held up his arms in defence and could have sworn he felt a brush of feathers against his forearm. One last screech, though, and the only sound was his own rapid breathing. Slowly, he lowered his arms again. Then he blew on his cold hands and rubbed them together. The joint, dropped along with his mobile, now lay on the ground alongside it, a faint glow still at its tip.

What the fuck were these pills?

So much for his nice, restful evening of getting high alone. He shoved everything into his backpack and headed back to the gap under the fence.

One thing was for sure – the coral pink pills would be going down Mum's throat from now on, and nobody else's.

<h1 style="text-align:center">TWO</h1>

Mum turned her hard stare on him as soon as he came into the bedroom, although her head remained on the pillow.

Those huge, round eyes should have given her a yearning and vulnerable look, like a Disney princess with a sleek, slug-like mane of hair. But instead they enhanced her defining quality: vigilance.

The muscles in the lower part of her left cheek quivered. In the series of croaks and mumbles that followed, Mark could just about make out his name.

It made him tense to hear her say it, even without the usual serving of weary mockery or frustration.

Oh, Mark. Almost all comments to and about him ended with his name. *You do realise trainers don't actually pick themselves off the floor, Mark? I cannot afford to pay your rent if you do not acquire a job of standing, Mark. I do not have to justify myself to you, Mark.*

The door to the bedroom clicked open. Mark didn't need to look up. He knew immediately it was Mum's friend Helen, just from the rhythm of her high heels on the linoleum floor.

As she sat on the other side of the bed from him, she dabbed at her eyes – outlined with their usual Elizabeth Taylor thick black eyeliner and twin slashes of purple shadow. She hadn't changed her look since Mum moved into the house opposite hers, fifteen years ago now. Ever since then, she'd been in and out of the front door, always ready for coffee and biscuits over gossip about the staff at the school. Technically, Mum was Helen's boss, but there'd never been much of the employer/employee dynamic about their relationship.

She stroked his mother's hand with what looked to Mark like a proprietorial air.

"You've got to get better, Marina," she said, in her best Very Sincere voice. "Then we can go and sit on the terrace and listen to the birds. You can make a rum and coke for us all."

Mark had to stop himself snorting at that. Not a fantastic idea, considering his mother's penchant for rum and coke was chiefly responsible for landing her here in the first place.

He'd always found it strange that *that* was her poison of choice. It didn't seem quite aspirational enough somehow: the coke bottles lined up like glaring red billboards among the middle-class pillars of balsamic vinegar and olive oil, the rum skulking guiltily behind them all. It was the smell he came to associate with home, always lingering under the ever-present wood polish, air-freshener and bleach.

"Dr Scott is right," Helen whispered, shaking her head. "She hasn't got much longer, has she?"

A week ago, his mother had at least been able to tell him how wretched she was feeling, even as he'd helped her to a cup of water. He'd never have guessed how hard it would be to help someone drink if they couldn't prop their head up on a pillow. Most of it ended up dribbling down the sides of her lips, which now had tight little creases at the sides, like knife marks at the edge of a pie.

You do realise I haven't been able to keep anything down for over two weeks now? You'd be crumpled up on the floor weeping if that happened to you, Mark. You need to be grateful you've got a trooper like me as a parent.

Well, the talking had mostly stopped now. More than a few sentences and she was out of breath.

Mark got the wireless speakers out of a cupboard – the ones Helen had bought for her, so she'd have something to listen to as she lay here, one hour dripping disconsolately into the next.

The speakers had a retro look: fake wood with big black cones. He put them on each of the bedside tables. "We've got you some music to listen to, Mum." The solicitous hushedness of his own voice sounded ridiculous to him.

Helen sniffed. "Well, keep it quiet. She's had a long day and needs to rest. I'm just going to fetch some coffee..."

After Helen left to go to the kitchen, Mark swiped his phone, looking for the kind of stuff Mum liked. When she was still with his dad, they'd listened to a lot of 60s shit, which he always found odd because they'd met in the 80s. But they had a whole load of Beach Boys CDs which they'd play on holiday car journeys; *God Only Knows* was their favourite. Mum would tap out the rhythm on the passenger-side dashboard with her fingers, while Dad would make an elephant sound for the whoop of the horns. They'd implored him to join in, but he never had done. Pity really, because that was pretty much the only time he could remember them being silly and happy together as a couple.

She'd switched to easy listening, after Dad had left.

He found an album cover with a moody monochrome

view of a city river viewed from a cafe balcony. *Retreat And Relax Jazz Collection.* Yeah, that sounded about right. Trombones farting lazily over saxophones drooling out long notes. He tapped *Play* and sank down into the chair next to her.

The music started with a slow pulse of bass guitar. Mark rapped a finger in time to it.

Looking down, he took a deep breath in.

Shit

There was an ant on the back of his hand: a huge one, abdomen gently rising and falling.

With a convulsion of disgust and fear, he got up, walked to the window and smacked one hand hard down on the top of the other. He lifted it to find the ant's long body broken – a series of dashes and commas. He noted the weirdly vivid dot of green on its thorax, a bit like the turquoise flash on a kingfisher, before brushing it away.

In the background, violins suddenly joined the bass – a long, mournful whine.

Fuck this.

He tore the cables out of the speakers and smashed them against the wall, again and again. Laughter spurted out of him in blasts with each blow. This was probably the closest he was ever going to get to the rock star guitar-smashing experience. Though the speakers weren't as robust as a guitar, and soon enough their electronic entrails had slithered to a heap at his feet.

"Mark!" Helen's voice from the kitchen, alarmed. "What on earth was that sound?"

The exhilaration drained out him. Deflated, he shifted the remains of the speakers to the corner with his toe and covered them with a spare towel.

THREE

Mark awoke the next morning to a buzzing in his ears. It was like a tiny insect was very, very close. Only it wasn't a steady continuous note – more like a code being tapped out, the rhythm tantalizingly familiar.

Sometimes, if he looked at a sunset or strong lights for long enough, he'd see a dark neon version of them flashing against his eyelids when he closed his eyes. And that was what the sound felt like – a sort of blaring echo projected onto his mind.

Tinnitus, it was called, wasn't it? He'd have to get it checked out. Strange, when he now spent nearly all his time around medics, he never had time to go to the doctor himself.

He hauled himself out of bed, cursing.

For some reason, Mum had set the bell to play Debussy, which she probably thought would be soothing, but Mark had come to loathe that delicate sprinkling of piano notes. He came crashing down the stairs in his boxers, intent on making it stop.

Through the opaque glass, he made out the blue

uniform of the district nurse – and, making a cursory effort to flatten his hair, he let her in. She nodded, said Hello, and then made her own way to his mum's room. It was downstairs now – a converted guest room.

He was about to go back upstairs when he felt a presence behind him, inducing him to twist around – and then groan at what he saw.

That fucking balloon again.

It was a huge helium one, in the shape of the number six, red with Santa-white furry tips and flirty eyes like Jessica Rabbit's on either side. The accompanying zero was hovering besides Mum's bed, all white with a snowman head on the top.

Helen had insisted they try to celebrate Mum's birthday last week. And make it Christmas-themed, because her birthday was 30th December.

"It's a milestone!" Yeah. Milestone. A great big stone round Mum's neck as she was drowning.

But Helen was the big occasion type and couldn't be satisfied with just a cake. She wanted decorations – bunting and tinsel and all the rest of it. Mark didn't see the point, when Mum wasn't able leave her bedroom any longer, but Helen had ordered the balloons nonetheless. The six had at first been attached to the ceiling. Inevitably, though, it had lost gas, and now it was floating round the house, bobbing up in odd places. Mark felt like it was stalking him.

He punched it, right in the middle of the eyes.

As it floated away, trailing its string behind it, the nurse called to him from the sickroom. "Your mum would like a cuppa, Mark."

Mark stumbled down into the kitchen, got it ready and stuck a straw in. He opened the door with his hip.

He turned round to look at his mother in her bed and

gasped. The cup smashed to the ground in front of him; he barely felt himself let it go as he slumped against the door frame. His throat went dry.

He was aware of the nurse, on the peripheries of his vision, following the direction of his eyes. But she didn't seem alarmed; just puzzled and concerned.

She walked over and stood beside him, a hand on his back. "Mark. What is it?"

Squeezing his eyes shut, he pushed the heels of his hands into the sockets. Then forced his head up again.

His mother was lying in bed, as he'd expected she would be. But her head was not where it had been. Instead, it was at least five feet above her body, on top of the mechanical arm of a crane.

The crane was perched on her torso, its lower lattices emerging like tree roots from the sashes of skin above her breasts. Not the entire crane, though – just the boom, from which her head protruded like a trophy on a wall, where you'd expect to see the pendant. It was like one of those telescopic cranes you saw sometimes on the back of a truck, bright red as a child's fire engine.

Boom and jib: strange words, remembered dimly from conversations with Dad, before the accident. Were they called that for a reason or did somebody just like the sound of them?

This was not what he should be thinking about right now. What was this? A bad trip after the pink pills? Had the crane appeared because he'd been thinking about Dad?

Mum's head was now straying from her bed.

"Please...," the nurse said quietly. "You've gone almost white."

"Something's... wrong with Mum." He barely croaked the words out.

The nurse raised her eyebrows at that. And he knew what she was thinking. *Yeah*, something was wrong with her. Four full stages of liver cancer, to be precise.

The boom advanced towards him, its sections slowly growing out of his mother's torso. It extended right over the bed, so Mum's face was now almost directly in front of Mark's, close enough for him to see the open pores and tiny blackheads on her nose. He planted his hands against the wall and closed his eyes again.

The nurse frowned. "Do you need to sit down, have a drink of water?"

"No. Thanks." Mark tried to keep his voice low, his breathing even. The last thing he wanted was someone reporting back to Helen about his mental health. "Sorry. I just think I need to get some air. The heat in here is making me dizzy."

The boom retracted, sliding back towards the bed. The sweat seeped through the neck of Mark's t-shirt.

"I'll open a window for you. Sit here. Let the blood run back to your brain and your vitals." The nurse put her hands on his shoulders and forced him down into the chair nearest the door. She patted his wrist. "I'll get you a drink."

Mark wanted nothing so much as to follow her out to the kitchen, so he wasn't left with... whatever *that* was. But his body had gone weak.

The boom extended upwards and outwards in his direction, bringing Mum's head to within a few centimetres of his own. It quivered obscenely, like a jack-in-a-box on a spring. Her skin was the yellowing-grey shade of a bruise in its final stages. Every so often, she winced and squeezed her eyes shut, with the pained expression of someone trying to loosen a well-lodged cork from the neck of a bottle.

The nurse arrived five minutes later with two glasses of water – one with a straw in for Mum, and one for him.

Mark took a sip and gripped it between his knees. There was that weird sound in his ears again – the buzzing. *Oh shit.*

He'd realised now why it seemed familiar. *Little bit of hash, a hand job and some POOOOOOOOOO-PPERS...*

It was the same rhythm as that bird song he'd heard in the woods. The same rhythm exactly.

He screwed his eyes up. He needed to talk to Simp.

FOUR

"Aw, Mark. Anyone can have a bad trip." Simp slapped his hands on the knees of his denim overalls.

Mark blinked at him. "A bad trip that lasts over twenty-four hours? Seriously? And I've got this weird buzzing in my ears. I can't get rid of it. It's like someone's tapping out Morse code in my head."

"Oh, that's nothing to do with the drugs." Simp waggled a finger at him. "There's a name for that, isn't there? Sounds like the name of a Roman emperor."

"Tinnitus?"

"That's the one."

"But what about the hallucinations?"

The old man pursed his lips, tossed a coin. "Pretty unusual, I grant you, at least ones that are so clear. But you're grieving, right? It's had an effect on you, psychologically."

Mark crossed his arms. "She's not dead yet."

"Yeah, but I meant, kind of pre-emptive grief."

Mark rolled his eyes. Simp had the unusual quirk, for a dealer, of lurching sometimes into California therapy-speak.

Mark was pretty sure he wasn't experiencing any kind of grief. But this wasn't like a bad trip either. He wasn't 'seeing things'. In fact, there were only two things he'd seen: those massive ants, and his mother's head on top of a crane. If he was having hallucinations, they'd be everywhere, not just at home and in the wood. Was there even such a thing as location-specific hallucinations?

"Simp?"

"Yeah?"

"Ever heard stories about that old scrapyard in Thurstrop Wood? You know the place – just behind those big fake Tudor houses."

"Hoo boy." Simp whistled and rocked back on the step he was sitting on. "You haven't been getting high there, have you?"

When Mark didn't answer, Simp croaked out a long laugh, his narrow chest heaving. "I made the same mistake once, lad. Looks nice and quiet. doesn't it? Rookie error."

"Do you know where all those metal insect things came from?"

"I do, as it happens. That was Robert Miles' old place. He was a handy man, dealt in a lot of scrap metal. We used to play pool at the Hind's Legs together on the odd evening. I remember when he first took that plot over. That big hump in the ground…" Simp traced the shape of the mound with his hand, cackling lasciviously.

Mark rolled his eyes. "That mound is weird. Do you know what it is?"

Simp stood up, and openly rubbed his backside. "Nah, but Rob's girlfriend used to festoon the blasted thing with ribbons and dance 'round it with flowers and shit. You'd have to have known her. Aurora, her name was. She probably thought it was the home of special fairy-sprite creatures or some such bull. Strange lass. Artist. She's the one that made them gigantic sculptures. I think she was inspired by Rob's insect collection."

"Huh?"

"Yeah. He kept them as pets in one of them sheds. All sorts – stick insects, exotic spiders, you name it. All in glass tanks. I always thought it a strange hobby for an odd jobs man. She must have used the bugs as models."

"There was a sundial type thing with a cricket sculpture..."

"Yeah, one of hers too. Bohemian sort, I suppose you'd call her." Simp rocked his head back and breathed out loudly, like he'd just had a long draught of beer. "She was *beautiful*. Always in those kaftan things and flares, but you could still appreciate the body. I could never see her without thinking of a butterfly. Really, really long hair. She dyed it blue. Loads of lassies do that now, along with the nose rings and tattoos and such like, but it was quite daring back then. As well as doing her art, she organised some special parties. I'm not talking kiddies' parties." He winked. "This was strictly for adults."

"Oh. Swingers, huh? How very 70s. Were you invited?"

"Tragically not, but I did hear all about them. It wasn't just sex stuff, mind. She'd do performances."

"Exotic dancing?"

"Nah. It was kind of like a parody of a kids' party. She'd wear a sexy clown outfit and do puppet shows and make things out of balloons to give to people. Only she wasn't doing poodles and giraffes, if you catch my drift." Another dirty laugh from the old man. "She was a bit of competition for me as well."

"Whoa." Mark laughed and held his hands up. "A

swinger and a sculptor *and* a dealer? You have no idea how cool you're making her sound here."

"I wouldn't call her a dealer, strictly speaking. No labs involved, or anyone else. All mushrooms and plants. Natural stuff. Lots of people called her a witch."

Simp knocked back his brandy and gasped, patting his belly.

"Do you think she was one?"

He gave Mark a weird little upside-down smile and grimaced. "Well, she certainly did a good disappearing act."

"You mean, she left Robert?"

A cloud passed over Simp's jolly, ruddy features. He bit his bottom lip. "Yeah. She left Robert, and Robert left… everything."

"Jesus. Suicide?"

"Nah. No way anybody could have done that to themselves."

"What do you mean?"

Simp broke eye contact and started scratching with a nail at the old painted lettering on the side wall of his house. It was at the end of a terrace, and had one of those old painted, fading advertisements for a barbershop.

There was a pub opposite, the Strangled Goose, which was where Mark had first come across him – part of a large chain, with the usual greasy laminate menus and crumbs all over the synthetic carpets. Mark had been doing a bit of bar work there over the summer, along with a few DJ nights, and Simp had taken an oddly paternal shine to him.

"All right." Mark sighed. "You don't want to talk about it. But you had a weird experience at the yard too?"

"It might just have been a bad trip. It was ants with me."

"Oh, fucking hell." Mark felt something shift inside

him, but he wasn't quite sure if it was relief or dread. "I saw them too. Were they really big, almost like spiders?"

"Aye, weird looking things. Proper gave me the willies. I was just sitting there, on a log. Got up for a moment and there must have been an entire colony of the little buggers crawling over my bare shin. A dot of green on each of the abdomens. Never seen anything like it."

"Yeah – the ones I saw had the same thing. Shit."

Simp held up a finger and shook his head. "Thing was, they weren't just crawling - they were making a *pattern*. You know those videos where people sprinkle powder on sensitive speakers? And when the music plays you get these shifting patterns appearing in the circles of powder? It was a bit like that. Long, dark lines of them." Simp shuddered. "There was this clot at the centre like a knot. And it was *pulsing*. When I got up, the ants all made off in little black streams down my leg and onto the log."

Mark shivered. "Perhaps that mound is a massive ant hill."

Simp nodded thoughtfully, and stroked his ratty little beard. "Could well be. People underestimate ants."

"The strength, you mean? They can lift the equivalent of a house on their back, can't they?"

"Yes. Not just that, though. You look at human evolution, and well, it's like a funnel."

Simp traced the shape of an egg timer – as crudely as possible, of course, the brown edges of his teeth showing as he grinned. "Seriously, though. All those homo-something species and most of them came to a great big dead end. But beetles and flies and ants... Well, their branch on the tree of life has spread out all over the place. So many routes to success. And they might not have our intelligence precisely, but you think how they can make decisions swarming together like that, guided by all that trial and error over the millennia." Simp shrugged. "In a face-off, I wouldn't bet against them, in all honesty. Cancer's named after the crab, but I often think ants would be the better comparison. The way they're all identical sisters in those nests, the way they multiply."

There were a few moments of silence, then Simp slapped his forehead. "Oh, sorry – that wasn't very sensitive, was it?"

"Fuck it, dude, chill. So, about these visions I'm having?"

Simp wagged his fingers. "Boy, I didn't tell you to take those pills. They were meant for your Ma. Might take a while to wear off."

"She wants some more, by the way. They're the only thing to get her to sleep now. They work better than the morphine."

"All right." Simp folded his arms against his chest. "Well, I suppose it's an act of charity to someone in that state. Anyway, I like you. You're a good boy, good customer. So, this is what I'm gonna do for you. Gonna give you some more of those pills for 20 quid, and I'll throw these downers in for free..." A snake-tongue flick of the eyes you always got with dealers, and Simp slipped him a little sachet of blue pills along with the pink shells. "One every four hours."

Mark stuffed the sachets into his pocket and took off, away from Simp and down the street.

"Don't think I've gone soft, Mark," Simp croaked after him. "I don't want to be hearing about none of all this from the rest of my clients."

FIVE

On the bus, on his way to the library, Mark shook a few of the downers out of the packet. Fittingly, they weren't as pretty as the pink shells. Just flat pale blue things that could easily be over-the-counter painkillers. He swilled two down with a bit of flat Lucozade from his backpack. The fuzziness on his tongue made a nice accompaniment to the ear buzzing.

He had a couple of hours before he had to get back and take over from Helen. What he was about to do would require concentration.

After he'd spoken to Simp, he'd got his phone out. First of all, he downloaded a bird call app. Later on, he wanted to identify that weird song he'd heard in the wood.

Then he sat back and googled Robert Miles. Inevitably, he got thousands of results, but when he entered the name of the town too, he found something relevant. A dead link to a blog. The title was still there, though. 'Weird Deaths in Britain: Robert Miles, 1974'

Mark felt a chill pass through him as he read it. Well, it

explained why Simp had tried to change the subject. What was so weird about this death, though?

This was the kind of highly localised news you needed a library for.

The bus was coming up to it now. He pressed the request stop button, the noise it made disturbingly similar to his mother's alarm, and winced as he swung himself around the pole to clatter down the stairs of the bus.

At the library door, he was greeted by a wave of air-conditioned cold that got him sneezing immediately.

Mum used to take him here every week when he was little. The kids' library was always noisy. He could remember when it had a brown carpet with orange octagons, not at all dissimilar from the one in The Shining, and probably hiding an atlas of stains. There was an oval depression at the centre of the hall, with steps leading down to a little nest at the bottom – a kind of amphitheatre of reading. Only, inevitably, the kids would use it to see how far down they could leap and land on the bean bags.

He wasn't allowed to do that, of course. Libraries, as far as his mother was concerned, were a place for reverence. She wouldn't allow him to talk above a whisper, let alone leap down steps. Every time they visited, he'd have to choose six books, all covered in some nasty, ratty plastic, and proceed quietly to the desk to have them stamped.

The library now was all pinewood flooring and blasé pools of white lighting. It was like IKEA, but with only one style of bookshelf available. In fact, there was more shelving and more brightly coloured wooden hills and trees than there were books. The place still had the Christmas tree up, with a little scattering of pine needles around it, the silver baubles somehow unspeakably sad beneath the strip lighting.

He made his way to the reference section. There was a bit dedicated to newspapers, all in file boxes, but the copies only went back six months. He'd have to ask someone if he wanted to dig any further into the past.

A woman stood at the desk. She had a gentle square of a face, rather weary.

BINITA, her name tag declared.

"Can I help you?" she asked.

"I'm looking for local newspapers."

"Oh, yes." She pointed behind him. "Just the shelves over..."

"Yeah. I saw those. I'm looking for something quite far back, though. From the early 70s."

"Ah." She rubbed her hands together, suddenly livelier. "You'll need to use our microfiche for that."

"Fish?"

She smiled. "Come on, I'll show you."

They went into one of the back offices, to be greeted by line after line of filing cabinets.

"Right," she said brightly. "So, is there a particular date you're looking for?"

"1974. I don't know which month it was, sorry."

"Gotcha. Are you happy to start with The Dreydon Examiner?"

It was the only local paper left standing in recent years. Mark nodded.

Binita opened a cabinet and looked through lines of labelled boxes. Finally, she took out an old-fashioned reel and led him to the microfiche, which looked to him like a very old computer.

She slid the reel over a peg, gently teased out the film and placed it over a glass panel. Then she hit Load. Immediately a screen full of old newspaper covers appeared. She showed him which knobs to turn to move forward and back-ward, zoom and focus – but the movements were jerky, and the pages of the newspapers slightly askew. A lot of the printing looked smudged, though pretty much legible.

Binita stepped backwards with a circular, regal wave. "I'll leave you to have a look now. Just come out and call if you need a hand."

"Thanks."

For quite a while, Mark found himself just flicking through what felt like endless minor crimes and scandals at the council and fairs. Finally, though, he caught sight of a headline that stopped his hand dead. 'POLICE PERPLEXED BY DEATH AT THURSTROP WOOD HOME'.

He scanned and found the name – Robert Miles, 42 – accompanied by a grainy photograph. Miles was a balding, thickset, ruddy man, his arms crossed over a shirt and tie; likely a guest at a wedding when the photo was taken.

At the bottom of the little column were the words '(Cont. p.4).' Mark turned the knob to get to the next few pages.

The next photo to appear made his stomach drop.

The young woman in the picture was in the foreground. She looked, in some ways, pretty typical of what you'd expect for the early 70s – very long straight hair, wearing flares and heavy wooden jewellery. But she also had her arms raised, to reveal a cape that was tied to both wrists and printed with the unmistakable pattern of a Red Admiral.

Didn't Simp say Miles' girlfriend had been like a butterfly?

The word suggested a fragility that wasn't right for her at all. There was a look in her eyes that Mark couldn't quite describe, a detached sort of glossiness. Just like an insect's.

The eyes did not, in any way, match the tightly controlled smile on her face, or the outstretched arms. As the shock wore off, he realised she was standing in front of some metal sculptures, all about waist height... a spider, a beetle and something with long spindly legs he couldn't quite make out. The beetle, he was pretty sure, was the same one he'd seen in the yard.

Slowly, his eyes scanned the print caption below:

Aurora Kent (age unknown), Mr Miles' girl-friend, an artist and party organiser, is pictured here with some of her sculptures. Police have been unable to locate Ms Kent since Mr Miles' death. They are asking anybody who had recent interactions with the couple to...

Mark looked further down the page, skipping ahead.

Mr Miles' remains were found on June 14th by children playing in Thurstrop Wood, who ventured into the scrapyard he owned, located behind his house. The coroner was unable to record the cause of death. The scrapyard had been closed and fenced off some weeks before-hand after being deemed a hazard. Detective Inspector Kenneth Felan...

Mark read through the rest of the article, but there wasn't really any more information about the couple; only interviews with bewildered neighbours.

He looked back at the photograph of Aurora. It wasn't just the eyes that disturbed him, but that smile. It had something of a model's under-the-eyelashes simper. But there was a bold blandness about it too, the kind you saw in corporate portraits. If she was in a suit, it was what you might get if you asked an AI to give you 'Employee of the Month'.

Suddenly, Binita bustled back into the room. "Everything going okay?"

"Yes, thanks." Mark pushed himself away from the desk. "I found exactly what I wanted."

"Well done you. Normally takes people a bit longer than that."

Mark looked blankly at the page before him, but he found he couldn't look at Aurora's eyes this time.

"Shall I take the reel out for you?" he asked the librarian dully.

"No, don't worry. I'll deal with that."

Mark was about to walk swiftly away from the desk, head swimming. Then, on one of the shelves next to the cabinet, he spotted a line of cassette tapes, all in bright red cases. There was a laminated note beneath them: STANLEY, DREYDON EXAMINER.

"Oh," said Binita cheerily. "That's quite the little archive there. Colin Stanley started out as the arts and culture editor and made his way up the ladder. Never recorded over a single interview tape, which is quite unusual. It's a regular treasure trove in there. He left it all to us after his death ten years ago."

She pointed at an old-fashioned tape player near the microfiche. "If you want to do some further investigations, you're welcome to play some of the tapes there. Honestly, it would be good to see someone make use of them. All of that labour and the tapes will probably degrade quite soon."

He shrugged. "Sure, why not?"

Binita showed him to the headphones, and he took down the box of tapes for 1974-5. All the cassettes had sticky labels on the front: mostly names he'd never heard of before, though he did recognise the name of a famous actor who'd lived in Dreydon for a while, for some ungodly reason. He was about to give up when he got to the final tape, and a sticky label that bore only one name: Aurora Kent.

Mark took a deep breath.

He sat down at the tape recorder, put the headphones on and slotted in the tape, hoping it hadn't already degraded.

Fortunately, the sound of static on pressing Play confirmed that it hadn't, though he had to fast forward a bit to get to the interview.

First a man's voice, deep but sounding tremulous and on edge. "Could you start off by telling me a little about your shows? How would you categorize them?"

Then a pause. The female voice that followed was rich, prickling with an arch, cold amusement. "I'm not sure there's a category that would fit?"

"Can you at least try? Having seen a slice of the show just now, I can already tell that this is hardly conventional puppetry. What influenced you?"

"Well, it was partly cabaret, I suppose. I am also a student of neo-paganism. My boyfriend keeps insects. I feel sorry for them, trapped in those glass tanks, yanked out of the colonies and nests they should be in. They deserve more respect from us paltry humans. The sculptures and puppets are an act of worship in a way. I have listened to those bugs with my recording equipment – much more sensitive than yours, I should stress. And the music that I use to accompany my shows is inspired by those sounds. You would not believe the orchestral richness all around us, which we are completely indifferent to because we are unable to tune into it."

"Fascinating. Would you have them available to listen to?"

"I suppose there's no harm in letting you hear a few of them. I wish I had a way to transfer them to LP..."

Some rustling and footsteps, followed by the tell-tale click of the cassette.

There followed some indistinct chirruping and rasping, barely audible. And then, a distinct rhythm that almost made Mark jump out of his seat: clean, crisp beats. It was far clearer than anything so far on the recording, including the voices of Aurora and the journalist.

Ting-takka-ting. Ta-ti-ta-ti-tee-tum.

It repeated several times. Mark found himself tapping a finger along to it – it really was a brain worm, like the beat on a trance track.

"Wow," the journalist breathed, once it stopped. "That's really quite remarkable. What insect is that? Can I hear again?"

Aurora's voice, again, suddenly abrupt.

"No. Sorry. That was a mistake. Could you make sure that tape is wiped? I can do that for you right now, in fact."

"But we'll lose the rest of the interview. I-"

The recording came to an abrupt, squeaky end.

Mark grinned. Never trust a journalist – the guy clearly hadn't deleted.

He rewound the tape and took out his mobile. Removing the headphones, he quickly recorded the insect sound that had so alarmed Aurora. It really was captivating – and with a bit of fiddling, he could make it fit for sampling. What with Mum going downhill, he hadn't been able to make any electronic music recently, which was pretty much the only thing capable of absorbing his attention in full. This would be a great excuse to get back into it.

He switched off the cassette recorder and walked to the door of the research room.

Binita looked up at him from the desk with that bland smile. "You managed to find what you wanted?"

"Not sure if it was what I wanted, but it was what I was looking for."

Her eyes crinkled up at the sides in confusion, but he could hardly start explaining. Instead, he nodded his thanks and loped away.

<h1 style="text-align:center">SIX</h1>

Mark paced the library, in search of something, anything, that would get that image of Aurora out of his head. Eventually he wandered upstairs, to the adult reference section. That, at least, would be quiet at this time of day.

Once he'd had a chance to sit at a table and breathe, he looked at his phone. 16.30. He had an hour left before the library closed and he had to go back and relieve Helen.

The buzzing in his ears, at least, seemed to be gone. The more he thought about it, the more absurd his reaction earlier felt. It wasn't *that* big of a coincidence. Why did he even give a shit about Rob Miles and Aurora and her weird little recordings of insects?

He needed to clear his mind. So, he might as well go and do what he'd originally intended and look up ants in the wildlife section. There was a shelf there devoted to entomology, and he swiftly found a book called 'Insects of Britain and Europe' – an old volume with filigree lettering on the spine. He took it to a table and placed it on the lectern to wade through. He looked up 'ants'; pored over the plates, with their delicate illustrations and labelled parts.

None of them looked remotely like the ones he'd seen in Thurstrop Wood.

He had a notebook in his pocket, along with one of those biros that you could switch colours with. In an effort to soothe himself, he started sketching one of the ant species that looked most similar to the ones he'd seen ambushing the jay.

He covered the eyes in tiny black biro dots, and then coloured in the abdomen with a green spot. He carried on until he had a good likeness, before putting it to one side, his notebook still open next to him.

He began to flick through the later pages, of ants' nests. All of them, he saw, had elaborate pathways. One was like a spindly branch, another a massive family tree, and one reminded him of that forlorn-looking Christmas tree on the lower floor – each layer of paths a little narrower than the last. Intricate enough to remind him of the structure of the brain.

After feasting his eyes on this for a while, he turned over the plates and came across another illustration. This time it was an ant carrying a larva. Next to it, a picture of a blue spotted butterfly clinging to a stem, its wings slightly ajar.

The Phengaris Rebeli butterfly is a brood parasite. It tricks the Myrmica Schencki species of ants into caring for their larvae through chemical signalling. It has been determined that they ascend in the social hierarchy through the use of acoustics, mimicking the sound of the queen ant. Only the real queen ant is able to identify the interloper.

He went back to his notebook and started, almost absent-mindedly, to sketch the butterfly, humming quietly. He couldn't get the light blue of its wings, of course, but he carefully drew the veins, and the dark dots at the border of the wing, that looked oddly like black-painted nails.

"Hey - Mark!"

Mark looked up. He knew that voice immediately – deep, with a slight lisp. It made him think of shiny, polished chestnuts, fresh from the shell. He looked up at Tom Souter, an ex-classmate of his.

It was the first time he'd seen Tom out of school uniform. Tall, broad-shouldered, good at sports, could easily have been best mate to a sexy jock in an American movie.

He'd had a string of girlfriends. Mark remembered the latest was a girl called Eloise, with strawberry blond hair and an upturned nose. Mark enjoyed the way she'd move among the desks, the little jolts of her hips.

But his eye snagged on Tom an awful lot more. And the thing was – Tom had looked back a few times.

With both men and women, Mark tended to go for the lanky, alternative types. But there was something about Tom's eyes... very large, and a slightly green-tinged shade of brown, like a damp log just beginning to acquire its moss. He had a very slow smile, and a dimple in a slightly unusual place in the left cheek.

Mark leaned back from the desk with a smile of his own, tilted his chin up and crossed his arms. "Oh. Tom. What's up?" He was surprised by the easy confidence of his own voice.

Mark was the quiet sort of delinquent. Not a hellraiser or a smooth rogue. So God knew where this self-assurance was coming from.

Tom raised his eyebrows, clearly a little taken aback. "Hi. I wasn't expecting to find you here..."

"Yeah. I mean, I'm barely literate, obviously."

"Hey, come on. Didn't mean it like that."

Tom did a kind of jokey burglar tiptoe towards him and leaned over to take a peek at his notebook. He whistled.

"Dude. That's not half bad. I never knew you could sketch like that."

Mark's instinctive response was sarcasm. He was about to reply with something scathing, when he looked down at the sketch of the butterfly – then at Tom's impressed face, then back down again at the page.

Damn it. It *was* good. He'd drawn idly, without really focusing properly. And yet somehow, he'd captured the felt fuzziness of the butterfly's wings perfectly with a biro. How?

"You should have done Art at school, Mark. You're good, man."

Mark said nothing, but traced the line of the butterfly's antennae with a finger. "It says here that it's a parasite. You don't expect pretty things to be parasites, do you?"

Mark looked up and gazed straight into Tom's eyes.

Tom's smile wavered a little at that. "I... I always thought that parasites would be little things, kind of burrowing..." He wriggled his forefinger. Suddenly, he seemed struck by the indecency of the gesture and his hand dropped. Mark laughed, way too loud, the sound of it echoing across the tiled walls. It was apparently infectious, because Tom slapped his shoulder and started laughing too. He was a rare example of someone whose laughter sounded good, and made him more attractive.

Tom seemed to get uncomfortable under that openly admiring gaze, and let out a little slip of a cough. "I'm really sorry to hear about your Mum, by the way. How is she?"

"Oh, she's fucked. Wholly fucked. I saw a scan of her liver. I mean, it looks more like an overdone steak. I give her about two weeks, tops."

Tom blinked and swallowed. "Oh God, mate. I'm so

sorry. She's such a good headmistress. So sympathetic, you know. Firm but fair."

Mark got up and stood in front of Tom, putting his hands on Tom's arms. "That's not true, though, is it?"

The other boy was startled. "What do you mean, not true?"

This sudden surge of power through the abandoning of the usual Sympathy Script was exhilarating. Mark leaned in, so Tom's handsome face was only a few inches away. "If you were a little too close to Mum in the last few months she was in the job, close like we are now, you could actually smell the alcohol when you went into the office. Years before that, she'd kept it hidden, but she was slurring her words by the time she got back home. She got a quiet word from the governors. It wasn't exactly a voluntary retirement."

Tom's face was flushed. "I'm... sorry. I shouldn't have brought this up."

Mark snorted. "Oh, look. There's no need to pity me. I'm gonna have a house soon, before I'm even 18. And no more drunken bitch of a mother. *I* was a parasite, as far as she was concerned. She made it clear, she resented each and every moment she had to take care of me rather than going on cruises and 'round garden centres in her spare time. Well, now she's leeching off me. My whole life is just a merry-go-round of medicine and nurse visits. And you'd better believe I let her know about it, before she went completely blotto."

Tom's huge eyes widened. "You're not in a good place."

"I'm in an excellent place, Tom," he said, enjoying the pressure of muscle against his thumb. "You want to join me there?"

There was shock in Tom's eyes, but something else too – excitement. "You were never like this at school."

He was right. Mark would never have approached any of the boys at school. Ever. His only stolen glances were at older men, hanging around outside shops and rail stations, their eyes speculative.

Perhaps it was being in such close proximity to death.

Mark was about to draw him in closer. But of course, that was the moment when Binita clattered upstairs. She gave Mark a nod of recognition. "Oh, hi. It's nice you stayed to do some further research. Just to let you know – we're 15 minutes from closing time."

Tom backed away from him quickly.

Fuck it. Mark ripped one of the blank pages from his notebook, scribbled his number on it, and slotted it into Tom's shirt pocket.

"Let me know if you'd like to take it further."

SEVEN

As soon as he walked into the house, the 6-shaped balloon bobbed towards him, then rotated in the air. Stupid thing. He had no idea why he hadn't pricked it ages ago. In fact, that was what he was going to do. Right there and then.

He went into the kitchen to find a pair of scissors.

And... *fuck*. There it was again. Right behind him.

He grabbed hold of it under one arm, preparing to sink the blade right into one of those eyes with the stupidly long eyelashes. But when he applied the blade of the scissors to the rubber, it just... yielded, much further than a balloon should do. It felt resilient; like a really plump sofa cushion pressed against a clenched fist.

Mark was frightened now, pins and needles in his fingers, but there was a rising, nervy anger in him too. He'd had enough of all this weird shit – at the wood, at home, in the library. This, at least, was one thing he could deal with. He could make this fucking thing burst.

Then he heard the giggle. It seemed a little muffled, as if it was in a neighbouring room. But it certainly wasn't his mother. She didn't have that kind of breath in her any longer, and it was too soon for any of the nurses.

The balloon escaped from his grasp. Scissors still in hand, he walked slowly down the hallway towards the kitchen. There it was again: that same giggle, with exactly the same cadence – low, feminine, conspiratorial.

"Is that you, Helen?" His voice was little more than a murmur. But he knew full well Helen didn't laugh like that either. There was no reply; just the heavy clank burring of the oxygen machines in Mum's room.

His hands were wet. He looked down to see blood trickling in several directions down his palm and wrist – a wonky scarlet spider. The scissor blade must have slipped.

Breathing fast, he stepped into the bathroom, found the box with the bandages, and started to wrap one round his hand.

And then another weird sound. A very particular type of squeaking this time – that muffled squealing sound of a balloon being twisted into shape.

"Hello?" he called. His voice cracked a little.

The squeaking intensified.

With an explosion of anger and fear, Mark burst out of the toilet. The balloon was in the doorway opposite him. It was bobbing near the floor now, contorting: like one of those party balloon animals being squeezed by a clown's hand, sprouting spindly new extremities.

Mark suddenly clocked its form: the 6 long, spindly legs easing out like knives from the thorax. An ant. A huge balloon ant, regarding him with two great, bulging compound eyes and its ocelli, rubber stretched tight like a mucous membrane.

Without warning, the bent legs powered forward, scuttling towards him at unfathomable speed. Backing up with a string of expletives, Mark slammed the toilet door shut behind him.

EIGHT

The rattle of keys from outside roused Mark from the trance of fear that had held him. How long had he been standing like that, back pressed against the toilet door? He was trembling; drenched in sweat.

It was Helen. It had to be.

Fingers tingling, he finally summoned up the courage to ease away from the door and open it.

The balloon was on the floor, crumpled and twisted. The only thing that distinguished it from a used condom was the flirty cartoon eye, which stared up at him, taunting. He scooped it up into a ball and marched to the kitchen, breathing hard.

Helen found him there, pressing the remains into the bin.

"Mark." Her voice was accusatory. "How long has Marina been alone?"

"Give it a rest, would you, Helen?" he snapped. "She's asleep. If she wanted something she'd press the buzzer."

Helen shook her head and filled up the kettle. She put a hand on the top of it and exhaled, hard.

"Since you're putting things in the bin – I saw the remains of the music system in there."

Shit. Mark never even looked in a bin when he chucked stuff away. Helen, though, was one of those people who just couldn't help 'noticing' everything – how long a neighbour's grass was, whether he had bags under his eyes, what was lurking in the fucking rubbish...

He sighed, put his hands over his cheeks. "Yes, sorry. One of the nurses knocked it over when she was cleaning up."

She crossed her arms. "That wasn't the kind of damage you could do by just dropping something. It had been smashed." She put the plastic bag on the kitchen counter and took out a cardboard box, and from the box another set of speakers – sleek, black and more robust looking than the others. "Please take better care of these ones. You can use them for your music too, if you like."

Mark didn't reply.

She sighed; put a hand on his back. "I know this is hard for you and it's unfair, losing your mum like this when you're so young. But really, it could be any day now. And you want to be able to look back on this and know that you made her as comfortable and happy as possible. You wouldn't want her to spend her last hours alone, or just with me."

Mark had to stop himself laughing bitterly at that. He was pretty sure Mum would be quite happy if Helen was the only one with her in those final moments.

But seriously, what was going wrong with his brain? Had he permanently fucked himself up with the drugs? He always thought that kind of thing was impossible, unless it was acid.

So it couldn't be that, could it? No – it was probably exhaustion, plain and simple.

"Mark – there was something I noticed when I was helping your mum on the commode..."

"I don't like the sound of this."

She rolled her eyes. "Oh, come on, quit the squeamishness... Look, have you noticed her back? There's a lump."

He shrugged. "Probably the liver, isn't it? Must be bigger than a duck about to be slaughtered for foie gras."

Helen took a deep breath, and closed her eyes. "I just think it's something we should flag up with the doctor."

When she said *we*, she meant him.

He rolled his eyes. "Fine. I'll give him a call later."

NINE

Mark entered his mother's deathbed room. It stank of bleach, as usual, but that wasn't what made him squeeze his eyes shut. He let the breath rush through his nose as he rubbed his forehead.

It was there: that fucking crane again. He found he couldn't even muster any proper fear this time. At least it moved slowly, unlike that scuttling balloon ant.

Perhaps he should take another one of those downers.

He opened his eyes.

The boom was still there, but it had retracted. It was a mischievous, playful thing, with something of the errant glove puppet about it. Perhaps it was there to grant his mother that spark of spontaneity she'd been so pitifully short of in life.

Where's your plan, Mark? Do you know the annoying thing about you, Mark? It's that you've never learned how to prepare properly.

The crane swung to the side, positioning Mum's face perfectly to look out of the window at the line of dull suburban houses over their back garden fence.

It was a pity this hadn't happened to her while she was still in good health. She'd have loved to spend her day craning (Oh Jesus - *craning*) her neck over her neighbours' walls. *I'm a people person*, she liked to claim. In fact, she was a dirty linen person, and the further her red drinker's nose was embedded in her neighbours' underwear, the better she felt about her own miserable excuse of a life.

Mark caught a reflection of his own face in one of the screens. He had the grudgingly solemn look of a small boy forced to sit through a long church service.

Back in the kitchen, Helen was bustling about, shopping bags on the floor.

"I'm just going to get some dinner ready for her," she said. When she said *dinner*, she meant *soup*. Because that was all his mother could take now. Even half of that ended up getting dribbled or vomited back up.

The microwave hummed its monastic chorus in the background.

"It's such a good thing Marina's able to be at home," she said quietly.

"Why?" he cut in. "She hates it here."

Helen looked at him in astonishment. "Why would you say that? She's more house proud than most I've met."

"Really? She bought everything here as cheaply as she could."

"So, she's thrifty. What's wrong with that?"

"Not just thrifty with money. Thrifty with love, joy…"

Skinflint. That was the word he wanted. There was something appropriate about it. She had a hind like flint: imperturbable and cold.

Helen shook her head. "I saw her happy plenty of times. That time we went to that wedding in Stroud? She was dancing the night away to disco music. This house is full of portraits of you both, beaming."

Oh yes: the yearly family portrait, always with some swirl of brown, gold and purple in the background. He was always made to wear a suit, and Mum would have her make-up on, and her special gold link chain. His grin got wider and more desperate with each passing year.

Helen sighed. "You're upset. You don't know what you're saying. You realise she might still be conscious, able to hear you?"

"We've got two shut doors between us."

The fact was, though, Mark hoped she could hear every word, every petty slight. She didn't just deserve his contempt. She deserved to *know* about it.

Helen closed her eyes. The lids had a dash of dark green today. "I'm sad, Mark. I'm sad that after all she did for you, you don't feel anything for her. It's the thing with mothers, you see – they do all the hard work, all the tough stuff. And then they get all the blame too. I know she could be pretty harsh..."

Mark slammed the glass down hard and lifted his eyes to the ceiling. "Helen, this isn't helping. She did her duty. But you could see how much she begrudged it. She saw me as a chore she had to do. A nasty, stinky one, like cleaning out the bin after a leak."

"Well, perhaps you should have tried to be a bit less of a chore as a human being, eh?"

Mark's shoulders sank. This was the trouble. There was a script for kids who had actually been abused, with wildly dysfunctional parents – taking a belt to them or refusing to feed them or making them sleep on urine-soaked mattresses or whatever. There were outlets. You were allowed to scream, post emotional stuff on social media, get therapy or whatever. But what about the more mundane reality of a parent who just... disliked you? Resented you? Who never just relished your existence and being? That was a First World problem, as far as most people were concerned. And filial gratitude and grief were the only acceptable emotional response. But he wasn't grateful, and he certainly wasn't sad.

Time to change the subject.

"Helen. Do you know much about ants?"

Helen's very well-waxed eyebrows rocketed up her forehead. "Eh?"

"You had the eco-club at school, Mum said. You built a bug hotel with them, right?"

He knew she used to trap moths and butterflies. She had a special box with a light. Once, when he was much younger, she'd shown him one of her hauls after she'd been out at a meadow. One of the butterflies had beautiful black and white wings, that reminded him of patterned lace stockings over pale skin. She told him that some butterflies have ears on their wings – little primitive chambers vibrating under the fuzzy surface.

"You must know at least a little bit about them?" he asked.

Her chest jumped with laughter. "Sorry. Yes. It's just such an odd thing to ask at the present time. I know a little. I wouldn't choose it as my Mastermind subject."

"The thing is... I think I might have brought back some weird species from the woods. By mistake. Anyway, I threw them out afterwards, but I did make a sketch. Can you take a look?"

She shrugged and sighed. "Why not, I suppose?"

He got his notebook out from a pocket and showed her the ant sketch from yesterday. Helen reared her head back in some surprise and clicked her tongue on the back of her teeth. "That's damned good, Mark. I didn't realise you could draw like that. You've got all the parts of the body there. And accurate too."

"It's a copy from an illustration. The green in the middle wasn't as light as that, more like the sort of green you get on a kingfisher. You recognise it?"

She grimaced. "Afraid not. You're probably best googling. Might be an invasive species... could cause devastation in the local ecosystem, like the Asian hornet. I know a few conservation groups you could contact."

She tapped her feet. Whenever she was thinking hard, she looked like she was waiting for a bus. "You said it was Thurstrop Wood where you think you saw them?"

"Yeah."

She pressed her lips together. "I've never liked that wood."

He nodded. "Because of the scrapyard, right?"

"Well, that's obviously an eyesore. Don't know why the council didn't tear that down years ago. It's not like there's a lack of families needing good homes. But I was more thinking about the wood itself. I used to take Trilby there most days, when she was still fit..." Trilby was her cocker spaniel, a once sprightly little beast that now had a wobbling gait and continuing spates of mange.

"Go on," he urged.

"I think it's something to do with the desire paths."

"Uh. The desire what?" Was this something to do with the cruising? If so, it was hardly the kind of conversation he wanted to have with Helen.

"The paths that haven't been clearly demarcated *as* paths. I mean, the wood's been organised as a grid system. The desire paths are the ones people take because it's a good short cut, or it's the natural route of curiosity. It's fascinating, there's been research that shows both people and animals will always go the same way. Anyway, in Thurstrop Wood, there's something... wrong with them. They're not where they should be. Oh, I don't know." She shook her head. "It's hard to describe. It just gave me a feeling of unease and disorientation. I was always getting lost there."

Mark wasn't quite sure how to respond to that. He could hear Mum groaning again. Then the buzzer went: the great belch of a sound that he'd come to loathe.

Helen frowned. "You'll need to take her dinner in and give her the oral morphine. I can't come in and see her right now, I've got a staff meeting to go to. Give her my love, would you? And Mark – please remember to call the consultant about that lump."

"Yes. Of course."

When Helen had left the house, he went back to his mother's room.

No crane this time, thank God. Just a body under the blankets, brown eyes open, chest moving slowly.

He put the tray with the soup down on the table next to her.

She moaned. Time for the pain killers again.

"All right, all right," he murmured. "Just be patient. I'll do it."

He found the bottle on the side, carefully measured out the liquid morphine. But Mum didn't open her mouth. Instead, she looked hard at him, her parched lips firmly closed.

He knew what she wanted – the pills.

"They're not doing you any good, those things, you know." A moan came back in response: high-pitched, pitiful. "Oh, fine." What harm could it really do her now, after all?

He found the sachet and carefully tipped out two of the pills, put them on her tongue, and helped her with the water. With a long, cathartic sigh, she rested her head on the pillow. He realised, too late, he should have tried to get some soup down her before she took the sedation.

He dangled the remaining pills in front of him in their sachet. There was one way of telling whether all this weirdness was to do with these or something else, he realised. One last experiment.

He took one of the pills out of the sachet, and swallowed it dry.

TEN

"Hello?"

"Good afternoon. Is this Mark Paisley I'm talking to?" The voice was surreally calm: plummy, male, middle class.

"Speaking." Less speaking, more croaking. Mark was shocked by the rawness of his own voice.

"Oh good. Can I talk to your mother, Mrs Paisley? Is she available?"

Well, was she? It occurred to Mark he had no idea how long he'd been asleep in bed. She could be dead, as far as he knew.

"She – she can't really have conversations any longer. She hasn't got the energy."

The voice slipped into the sympathy tilt he was so familiar with. "Oh. I see. I'm sorry. I can perhaps talk to you instead for a few moments? I'm her solicitor, Donald Harley, of Harley and James Partners? The thing is, Marina is currently intestate. Which would mean that on her passing, all of her estate would pass to her husband, your father. And they've been separated for some years, as I remember."

"Dad? We don't know where he is, even."

"Right. Well. It would be good if we could have something concrete on that. The estate will, of course, be passed on to you if he doesn't come forward to claim it. But it could make acquiring the probate quite difficult and time-consuming, which I'm sure you want to avoid right now."

The conversation lingered on for a bit, with a fair degree of bloated sympathy and legal jargon, until Mark agreed he'd try and find out exactly what had happened to his father.

His hand lingered on the phone after he'd set it back down into its nest.

Mum sometimes said he was a deadbeat, just like his dad. Mark actually liked that word, 'deadbeat' – it was what you should call that moment in a drum and bass track, just before the beat dropped.

His dad hadn't always been a deadbeat, though. Not until the accident.

The company had paid all the costs, but the aftermath seemed to unpick the knot of Dad's habitual calm. He did not, like Mum, resort to drink. But he'd disappear for days on end, returning with an odd, distant look and the smell of smoke on his breath, leaves and seeds stuck to the woollen coat he always wore in winter.

When he did return, often late in the evening, Mum would stand in the kitchen, always with her arms wrapped round her own chest in a very tight hug. A gesture that from anybody else might have suggested vulnerability, but with her was always a sign of an imminent explosion. Mark stayed in his room, Dad's voice too low for him to hear the answers to her fierce jabs of questions.

Eventually, though, he'd hear the familiar creak of the

stairs as Dad made his way up – always the same distinct, faltering rhythm. Then there'd be the creak as he lay on the bed and switched on his music, the volume loud. As the old country and western tracks filtered down the stairs, Mum would smack the pots and pans together as she washed up. She could do angry, noisy housework better than anyone Mark knew. She had martyrdom down to a rage-polished tee.

One day, after Dad had been out for hours, she put all his stuff out on the lawn. It wasn't like in the movies, with lots of screaming and tossing things out of windows. No, she did it with all the solemn sense of order she put into packing stuff in the boot for their caravanning holidays, everything perfectly slotted in like Tetris blocks. When Dad came back, he didn't beg or cry or rage. He just took his immaculately piled boxes, stuck them in the car and drove off.

For a while afterwards, Dad did visit him periodically. Mark found his guilty taciturnity easier to bear than Mum's relentless wall of righteousness.

At first, they went birding together. Before the accident, Dad had been meticulous – he always took his field book, and would note down each bird in a special notebook, along with the co-ordinates. Afterwards, he'd just hand Mark the binoculars and idly flick through the field book, his face set to the sun and his eyes closed.

Eventually, Mark suggested they just go out for lunch instead. It was a decent enough excuse both to see Dad and to get the kind of junk food he was never allowed at home.

The last time they'd met up, Mark had just turned 13. Dad hadn't sent a card or phoned on the day, but he did bring a present with him to the café – a new field guide for birds. Mark harrumphed a thanks before putting it straight in his backpack.

As they were waiting for food, Mark brought a yo-yo out of his pocket.

"You seem a little old for that now," Dad said, without rancour. He had shadows and lines under his eyes then, so deep they looked like those curtain sashes you got at the top of windows in posh houses.

"Mum thinks it'll cure my fidgets."

He'd lifted the yo-yo and let it fall from the string. It lit up in red and blue when it twirled.

The only sound was the coffee machine hissing away in the background. The cafe owner had her hand on the phone, not looking at the pair of them.

Dad's eyes, gummy and shot through with red veins, rose to meet Mark's – and for the first time in a while, he hadn't looked detached. He'd taken Mark by the sleeve and dragged him out of the cafe.

It was raining, and they were both immediately splashed by a car dashing past. But Dad ignored that. Just kept grasping at Mark's the sleeve, drawing him close.

"Your mother told you what happened?"

"What, at the site?"

"What else would I be talking about?"

Mark had shrugged. "She said there'd been an accident. That it was the company's fault, not yours."

Dad looked down, licked his bottom lip. "It was easy to make out it was partly Craig's fault, partly the result of bad procedure. But it wasn't the company. Wasn't him either. We took turns to do the checks before we started the work. Craig's full name was Craig O'Grady, but his nickname was Craig O'Seedy. Not because he was the creepy type – it was O'Seedy for OCD, because he was real careful with anything safety related. Paranoid, even. He'd have to test all the brakes at least twice. He'd lock, unlock, lock and unlock again. No way he'd get anything wrong. Anyway, it was my turn that day. I went through the list, but someone distracted me – some bollocks about getting palettes down from the delivery truck. And I never checked. We just got into the cabin together, in a rush and all.

So it went up in the crane, about two hundred feet or so. We were about to lift the load, and Craig asked me to stop just for a moment so he could have a fag. He leaned out of the window, and it just... clicked open. Then the door was flapping wide open and I was staring out at this emptiness... this blue expanse. Oh God, Mark the sky was so blue that day, not a cloud out there. And it happened so quickly. There was a scream, all the way down, and then..." Dad screwed his eyes shut. "It's true what they say about the sound of a body hitting the ground from a great height. Just like an egg cracking. I couldn't stop myself looking down. He was face up."

For a few moments, they'd just listened to the rainwater dripping from the eaves.

"I don't know what I'm doing here, Mark. I need to get away. I need to get you and your mum out of my head before it's too late."

Mark blinked at him. "What do you mean? Why would you want us out of your head?"

Dad ran his hands through his thinning, white-streaked hair. It had been as black as the ravens he had loved, up until a few years ago. "It's not because I don't love you. The opposite, in fact. If I go, as far away as possible, she might not be able to..." He trailed off, lifted his eyes to the sky, which had the pregnant grey heaviness of a day of deluge.

Mark was vaguely aware that this would be a good moment to cling to his father; protest that he did need him and plead for him to stay. But that just seemed ridiculous, a scene from a straight-to-TV movie.

Instead, he just watched as Dad walked away down the street, the rain battering that waxed jacket he always wore, giving Mark not one single backwards glance.

ELEVEN

He needed a few hours' distraction, Mark realised. So he got out the laptop and his mobile phone and had a go at recording the insect riff from the recording.

He managed to strip it of most of the buzzing and crackling until it was fairly sharp, deciding as he did to start the track just with the rhythm – a stripped down beat that sounded a bit like fingers tapping on a table.

Then he added some padding – a silk skein of synths, a hint of pipes.

And finally, a little of his own vocalizing, but no distinct words.

He listened back: it was just a little bare, still, but that beat was still hypnotic.

He saved it.

What would be a good title for it, though? He quite liked that name of the butterfly he'd researched at the library. Phengaris.

Phengaris Blues, then. A good name for a track.

And now, he needed to check on Mum.

TAKING A DEEP BREATH, he got a firm grip of the door handle, then pressed it down and stepped inside the death room. She was still sleeping. No crane.

So, it seemed Simp's downers had finally worked their magic. Or rather, un-magic.

There was no point waking her up now. He might as well go upstairs and have a look for some of the documents she kept under the bed before she woke up naturally and started demanding soup and sedation.

Opening the door to her bedroom, it struck him that he hadn't been in there since she'd stopped being able to get up the stairs.

It was an immensely tidy eyesore – smoothed quilt, artfully placed cushions, all in yellow and queasy green, with curtains to match.

She had one of those beds with an end lift and storage units under the mattress. That was where she kept all the documents. He found the strap and pulled it up on its metal hoist, the movement producing a groan impressive in both pitch and length.

Once, when he was a toddler, he'd watched Mum open the bed like this. She hadn't noticed he was in the room. He put his neck directly under the mechanism, but she'd noticed just in time, before putting the mattress back down. She always claimed afterwards that, were it not for her vigilance, he'd have been beheaded.

At least that way you'd have an excuse for being a brainless hunk of meat.

And always followed by that awful laugh of hers – never a peal of giggles, but a single, ugly blast.

It was mostly bed sheets and towels under there now, all

perfectly folded of course. But quickly enough he found a likely-looking box, full of yellowing old birth certificates and family albums. He flicked through, but there was nothing in there about Dad, other than their marriage certificate.

Then he saw the envelope – Last Will and Testament. She'd actually done a copperplate type job with the hand-writing. Well, that would make things easier. He'd just hand it over to the solicitor.

It hadn't been sealed, so he decided to have a quick look inside.

'I give and bequeath to Helen Farrion, should she survive me, all funds in my savings account and ISA. I give and bequeath all of my personal effects and house to my son Mark Paisley, or if he should predecease me, then to Helen Farrion.'

Mark smiled wryly. She never wanted to give him any money directly; always said he'd spend it on the wrong things or become even more workshy than he already was.

He was about to lower the bed again when he noticed another box next to the first one. It looked like the papers inside were quite new. He pulled it out; one of the letters at the top blew off the top and landed at his feet.

He instantly recognized Helen's handwriting from the Post-it notes she used to leave on the fridge for Mum. He'd know those weird little sashes between the dots of the i's and the great whiplash loops anywhere.

Weird she'd written a whole letter to his mother, though, when she lived across the road and they spent prac-tically all their time in each other's living rooms.

He was about to put it back in the box, then thought twice; pulled it out, and smoothed it down.

Sod it.

Helen had told him to fetch this thing, so how much of a violation was it really?

DEAR MARINA,

I'm sorry we quarrelled. I cannot bear to think of you angry with me. I simply want to breathe in the scent of your hair. I've never known anybody with quite such a mane of silky black. When I press my cheek to it, it's as if I'm in a cool forest, my head on a mossy log, surrounded by bluebells. It's a lace-like scent, so faint and yet so complex in its layers. I close my eyes and I can taste you, that deep spiciness I like to roll around my mouth after I've had my head between your legs. I'm wet just thinking about the yield of your belly and the softness of your thighs. Velvet, satin and silk. Don't ever think there's a shame in that tenderness. And just think, next week I've got time off booked and Mark's at school. We can't sacrifice that precious time we'll have together.

HE SLAMMED DOWN THE LETTER. There were more of them, he saw, looking at the box – same writing, same paper. A sheaf of letters tied up with a red ribbon.

At first, he was stunned. Then he started to laugh – and, once it sputtered out of him, found he just couldn't stop.

He closed the bed and sat down on the mattress.

Mum would turn of the TV if there was a gay kiss on a soap. She wanted respectability, No Nasty Talk from the neighbours or her colleagues. It had never occurred to him to try coming out to her.

He inhaled deeply, then started laughing again, harder. Deep, guttural, filthy laughter – the sort you sometimes heard from women in bars who clearly had deep and entangled roots of friendship and filthy confidences.

TWELVE

Pink wisps followed the pills as Mark swilled them down the sink.

That was it: no more uppers. No more downers. At least not for now.

Helen had come that morning. She was bustling around as usual now, making porridge and tea. He leaned on one of the kitchen cabinets.

Eventually, she wrinkled her nose at him. "Mark, is there something wrong? You've been looking at me in such a strange way."

He took a deep breath in. Not the time to bring up the letters – he didn't have the energy. Not today. He had other business he needed to resolve, though. "Yeah. Actually, I need to know something. A solicitor was in touch yesterday and there are things that need settling. So, I'm going to have to be blunt here. What happened to Dad?"

Helen paused. For a woman with such an expressive face, and the sort of bright make-up that emphasized it, she did Inscrutable surprisingly well.

"Oh, come on. I saw the looks between the pair of you

when his name came up. You were keeping something back."

After a pause, she gave a slight nod. "Yes. This should come from your mum, really. But I don't think she can any longer."

"Can what?"

She sighed. "Come on, we'll go to the dining room table."

It felt oddly like an interview: her on one side of the table with her coffee cup, and him on the other. She took a sip and picked at the elbow of her dress. It was black, covered in white roses. She was wearing pearls, too. It occurred to him that she dressed rather older than her fifty-five years, although there was always a certain glamour to her. Mum had always been into film noir; the Hitchcock blond heroines. Perhaps that was what had drawn her to Helen.

"Look," Mark said, scratching the top of his head. "There's no reason to be like this. I know he was running away from something. Probably the law, right? Otherwise, why would he have cut all contact like that? He didn't want me and Mum implicated..."

She laced her fingers together. "As far as I know there was nothing of that kind. It happened a few years after you last saw him."

"*What* happened?"

Helen's eyes dropped quickly. She took a breath. "His death, Mark. I'm sorry."

Mark slumped back in the chair. His tongue felt oddly fuzzy, but what really got him was how muffled his emotional response was. He was vaguely aware he should shout, scream, demand to know why he hadn't been told this. But he simply waited for her to carry on.

"It was suicide."

He breathed in sharply, his fingers grasping the fabric of his jeans.

"What? When? How long have you known this?"

"He was abroad, somewhere in South America, I think. Marina was informed by a policeman over the phone, one who didn't speak English terribly well. Not the best way to find out." She rubbed her forehead.

"Oh, not the best way? Do you think? Do you think it's worse than this way?" His anger was sudden, hot and dry.

Helen winced. Her eyes travelled to the window, where the Astroturf gleamed in front of the patio. There were some sparrows on the fence, though God knew what they thought they were going to find there. "I don't know what to say to you," she said. "I did tell Marina she owed you the story. But I suppose it was just too painful."

"*Painful?*" He scraped a hand through his hair. "Marina, there was no pain. She hated him. I mean, not quite as much as she hated me, but something pretty close to it. She was glad he left. She was just too much of a coward to tell me straight up. Or maybe she didn't even think it was important enough."

He waited for her to contradict him, but she kept her eyes on the window.

Mark lowered his forehead to the table, and felt the coolness for a little. "Do you know how he did it?" he asked eventually.

"If you must know..." Her throat undulated a little as her eyes met his again. "He was still working on building sites. He hanged himself from a hook on a crane."

Mark quickly got up off the chair, so fast it fell down.

Dad's face staring at the upturned yo-yo came back to

him suddenly, startlingly clear – those glazed eyes reflecting the blue and red lights.

Helen tried to grasp his hand. There were tears suspended in her eyes now, something close to a pleading expression. "There was just no gentle way to tell you. I'm sorry. I just wasn't expecting this, or I would have planned more care-"

"Fuck's sake. I need to get out of here."

"You shouldn't be on your own. Not in this state."

But Mark backed off, his hands held high as if in surrender, head shaking rapidly. He had to go – somewhere, anywhere away from here. Away from the house.

THIRTEEN

He shivered in his duffel coat, wishing he'd put a hoodie on as well. Although it had long stopped snowing and the sun was shining, the wind was strong and chilly. With his mother's condition, he'd got used to having the house at sauna-like temperatures.

He was heading towards the shopping parade a few streets away from the house – though 'parade' seemed too grand a word for what was basically a post office and a couple of hairdressers. But it also had a betting shop with a video game arcade, and they rarely asked for ID. Going in there was the most obvious way to get the image of the crane and straining rope out of his head.

His phone began to vibrate. He got it out of his pocket and swiped.

A text message, from an unknown number.

Want to meet? T

He thrust the phone right back into his pocket. His first impulse was to ignore it. But then he remembered Tom's brown eyes, those oddly placed dimples when he smiled.

They had to be a more effective distraction than flashing lights and the clatter of coins from the fruit machines or the looks of furtive men shuffling up to the bookies.

He rested against a front garden wall and took out the phone again, tapping at the keypad and wishing he had a pair of gloves to put on afterwards.

2day?

The reply appeared in its little blue bubble with a pop, almost immediately.

Are you at home? I know the street.

Oh, no way was he taking Tom upstairs. Not while Helen was down there with Mum.

He quickly thumbed out his reply.

Got to keep the house quiet. U near Thurstrop Wood?

———

THE PAVEMENT GLITTERED with an eczema of salt scattered the night before, which crunched under Mark's boots.

His tinnitus had come back and seemed to be intensify-ing. It was more like a steady, muffled thump now – the kind you get when you hear someone playing music with a heavy bass through a wall. He tried to treat it like a beat to distract himself, jogging along to it down one of the paths.

Tom was already at the pond where they'd agreed to meet when Mark arrived. He seemed uncharacteristically nervous: one leg bent, leaning against the tree. It was a self-conscious, model-like pose. Adorable, but probably not the way Tom thought it was.

Mark walked right up to him, put one hand against the tree trunk, and reached a hand around Tom's neck, rubbing a finger against the soft, short hairs just below the longer layers. A mild buzz of alarm sounded at the back of his mind; he didn't have a huge amount of experience with foreplay, but he'd certainly never gone in for long embraces. The unfamiliarity, though, was exciting.

He leaned in and kissed Tom, slightly just above his lips, before tilting his head one way to start properly making out.

He could tell Tom was unprepared, because his lips didn't give way immediately. Quickly, Mark slipped a hand under his hoodie and t-shirt, feeling the warm flesh under the boy's navel and the hair, and began to dig under the elastic of his tracksuit bottoms.

Tom gasped in pleasure – then grabbed Mark's hand, holding him back. "Whoa."

Mark broke away; cupped a hand under Tom's chin. "What? We didn't come here to have a nice hike, did we?"

Tom's eyes darted from side to side. "Sure, but..."

Mark took a pace back, his arms spread. "I mean, who cares who sees us, right? You reckon they're going to do anything but hurry on by, muttering into their scarves?"

Tom crossed his arms against his chest.

"Oh look. If you really are that nervous, I know somewhere I can *guarantee* nobody will see us, all right?"

———

AS THEY WALKED to the scrapyard, Mark grabbed Tom's hand, and the other boy did not resist, although he didn't squeeze back, the nervousness not quite leaving him.

After they'd got through the hole in the fence, Tom blinked at the sculptures. "Wow. I can't believe this shit. Who did it?"

"An artist lady who used to live here with her old man.

Anyway, the place is supposed to be haunted. So, let's go ahead and scare the ghosts."

Mark laid down his coat on one of the logs, then pulled off his jumper and shirt. The wind struck him hard across his bare back, but the sensation seemed to do nothing but add strength to the tingling of his body.

They embraced again, Tom's hand tracing a long curve across Mark's back down to his buttocks. The peculiar patchwork warmth of Tom's body against his, combined with the punishing wind against his back was adding to Tom's excitement. The song from the wood pigeons seemed to intensify, along with the sound of the wind in the trees up above and the shuddering call of a tawny owl.

Mark pulled back and took hold Tom's lapels, pulling him towards the mound. It was waist height, perfect for bending someone over...

But just as they got there, Tom began to slap at his own face. "Fuck, it's a wasp. Fucker just stung me."

"Can't be. This isn't the right time of year for bees..."

But Tom wasn't wrong. It was indeed a wasp. Mark watched as the creature meandered away to die. There were several more, though: all circling around Tom's head, buzzing angrily.

"Have you got something sweet on you?" Mark asked.

Tom's forehead furrowed. "Huh?" Then howled, suddenly, and slapped the back of his neck.

MARK STARTED SWATTING at them too, but they just looped back to Tom, who fell to the ground, arms covering his face. "FUCKING DO SOMETHING, MAN!"

Mark looked around. The wasps were coming from the

mound, he realised. They crawled round it in oddly dense streams. It was like a helter-skelter, with a moving river of wasps for a slide.

Without really thinking about it, Mark started to whistle in rhythm to that song, *his* song. *Little bit of hash, a hand job and some POOOOOOOOOO-PPERS*

The churning river of wasps seemed to coagulate, then came to a halt, along with their buzzing. Mark clapped his hands – and in an instant, the wasps flew off, in all directions.

He returned to Tom, kneeling beside him.

"You got many stings?"

Tom just groaned.

Mark put a hand on his arm. Instantly, Tom rolled away from him.

"No." There was real fear in Tom's eyes now, and something pretty close to hatred. Mark seized him and managed to get his mouth to his neck, pressed his teeth against the skin. But this time Tom pushed him hard enough to make him topple backwards onto the ground.

"I swear you touch me again and I will knock out some of your teeth," Tom yelled.

Mark lay there for a few moments, then levered himself up on his elbows, laughing.

"Come on. At least fuck me. It can be a hate fuck. You don't do it now, you'll just go back to your girlfriend and have lots of vanilla sex and you'll never know what it's like."

Tom shook his head. "Fucking freak. What did you do to those wasps?"

"What did *I* do to them? What do you think I am, Tom? Candyman?"

"I've no idea. Not sticking around to find out." Tom got

to his feet, clutching one of his arms, and quickly scuttled towards the hole in the wire fence.

Mark was shocked by how melodious his own laughter sounded, rippling out across that cold yard.

FOURTEEN

The voice he heard behind him as he crawled out under the wire fencing was plummy, feminine, casual. And he recognised it immediately.

"I see you, Mark Paisley."

He'd listened to Aurora for all of about two minutes on a scratchy recording. And yet he was sure he'd never forget that tone or timbre.

He turned round in a slow circle, his heart pounding, sweat quickly soaking his collar, the giddiness he'd felt with Tom dissipating in an instant.

"Where are you?" he shouted.

In response, that same low giggle he'd heard in the house when the balloon transformed.

His eyes were drawn to the polished surface of the sun dial. He caught a brief glance of his own pale, terrified face. And then he noticed, below the pointer, something moving. Slender feelers like black pipe cleaners reflected in the brass – moving purposefully, as if searching for a signal. Then a narrow, dark head, antennae quivering above it.

Fuck. It was the grasshopper: the wrought iron one

trapped between the pointer and the sundial. Now come to life.

It leapt onto the ground and scraped its front wings together, the resulting noise nothing like the gentle chirping stridulation Mark had heard in gardens in the summer. Instead, it was unbearable, a creaky metallic whine.

Its hinged legs flexed. The movements were jagged, but it was still terrifyingly fast. After a second jump, it was standing just a few feet from Mark.

Its compound eyes glittered as it regarded him, head-on. It bent down low, clearly ready to pounce.

"Oh, Mark." Aurora's voice was lush, coddling. There was not even a touch of malice in it. "Don't you like my adorable pets, my love?"

Mark didn't wait to find out if it had enough power in its legs to reach him.

FIFTEEN

Once he was back in the wood, panting with his hands on his knees, Mark vomited: more than once, the fluids spattering his trainers.

Then he heard that same bird song again.

Little bit of hash, a hand job and some POOOOOOOOOO-PPERS...

Fuck this. He was at least going to find out what that was.

He got out his phone, found the app he'd downloaded earlier and held it up in the direction of the song.

For a while the search function performed its predictable whirling. Then:

No match for any bird known in the British Isles. This could be because of poor sound quality. Record again?

Big fucking surprise. Mark was ready to close the app and shut his phone down. But then he walked a little further and recorded a different song. This one, he thought, might be a robin – it had that kind of intricacy and volume. But when he recorded it...

No match for any bird known in the British Isles. This could be because of poor sound quality. Record again?

He spent a good fifteen minutes with quivering fingers, desperately recording different bird songs, but not one was recognised by the app. Eventually, he logged off. Probably a glitch, he thought.

He noticed a WhatsApp message from Tom, but ignored it, shutting down his phone. That wasn't a conversation he needed right now.

———

ONE OF HELEN'S Post-Its was on the fridge back home.

I'm really sorry about upsetting you earlier.

A queasy contraction twisted in his gut. Fuck, how was three years' late news of his father's suicide the least traumatic thing that had happened to him today?

In retrospect, I should have thought of a different way to tell you. Marina did make sure to give me your father's death certificate. So you don't need to worry about the legal stuff. I'll be back tomorrow. Remember to call Mr Singh about that lump.

Singh was his mother's oncologist.

Mark had to laugh. Typical Helen. The impulse to chide was so strong, she couldn't restrain herself even when she knew she was in the wrong.

He went into the bedroom to check on Mum. All was pretty much as normal.

Helen had turned her over to lie on her front. That was routine – she had to be turned this way and that regularly to prevent bed sores erupting. But the back of her night dress had been parted to reveal the lump. And Jesus, it *was* huge – a great big mound of a thing.

He covered her up again and went upstairs to call Singh. He wasn't on hold for long.

"Mark... how are you?" There was a careful professional sympathy in Singh's voice. "I'll just bring your mother's records up... Oh yes. Are you satisfied with the care from the nurses? Do you think she might need some more in the way of carers?"

"No, no. It's all fine. It's not about that. Mum's got a growth in her lower back. We need to get it checked out."

There was a pause. Just the hint of a sigh. "Mark, I don't think there's much point in that. The journey in the ambulance would be very painful and distressing for her."

"Well, yeah. But having a tumour that size is pretty stressful too. It's bad, you know. It's making it impossible for her to sleep on her back.

"Okay, well, you'll need to shift her onto her side regularly, then, to avoid the sores and..."

"But shouldn't we actually check it? X-rays, scans, you know?"

This time, the sigh on the other end of the phone was loud and pointed. "You're quite right. It's likely to be a cancerous growth. But it hardly makes much difference at the palliative stage. And your mother specifically requested home hospice."

Mark knew all of this, of course. He had been given the spiel by the nurses: dignity, options available, blah, blah.

"Are you okay, generally, Mark?" Singh asked, no doubt trying to be caring. He just sounded weary, though. "I know your mother's friend has been supporting both of you."

Mark had to grin at that. "Yeah. She's been a real brick. But, you know, it's tough being with Mum at the end."

"I know. You're so young as well. And it's hard to see someone who was once so strong deteriorate..."

Mark used to hate the sort of clichés people churned out in hospitals and at funerals, but he could kind of see the point of it now. It allowed people to glide around on the icy surface of interaction without fear of a plunge.

So he happily *mmmmd* and *ahhhhd* his way through the rest of the conversation, even when Singh earnestly told him that many family members in his position felt it a privilege to be there for their loved one right at the end.

Luckily, Singh's voice started to acquire that finishing cadence shortly after that. He assured Mark he would contact the hospice and make sure some palliative care nurses were sent 'round soon.

Mark even made an effort at a tearful voice at the end of the conversation. What would it look like to Singh otherwise?

Christ, Tom had told him he had changed. But perhaps it wasn't the glorious shedding of a carapace. Maybe it was a regression, a folding back into a cocoon of fear and social caginess. The one Mum had been trapped in all her life.

SIXTEEN

Once he was back sitting next to Mum as she slept, Mark took out his phone and brought up Google. Apprehensive, he thumbed 'Craig O'Grady building site death' into the search box. The result was immediate – a couple of reports from local papers after the incident and a few behind paywalls about the legal aftermath.

He started searching for an obituary, and found an online memorial.

Craig O'Grady. Beloved son, brother, colleague and friend. 1954 - 2016

Mark skimmed the rest of the page. It was what you'd expect for the most part. Craig had been born in Arizona. Active, outdoorsy type, good at baseball. There were some jokes about his obsessive tidiness. He'd moved to the UK for an apprenticeship and then got married to a British woman in 1980. No kids.

Mark was about to scroll away when something caught his eye and made him gasp.

It was a picture of Craig with a group of other builders, most of whom were in hard hats and high-vis. Craig was clearly young – hardly out of his teens, skinny and bare-chested and grinning. But that wasn't what made Mark look twice. It was one of the other men standing next to him. He instantly recognised the ruddy, middle-aged complexion and the tight smile.

Shit.

Mark held his phone close. And yes, it was clear: that was Rob Miles.

He took a few deep breaths. Okay. Miles was a general handyman, so it wasn't really surprising he was on building sites.

He was leaning on Craig's shoulder with his elbow, though. It looked like they were friends.

And it occurred to Mark – if Simp knew Rob, he might have come across Craig too.

———

HE WENT to Simp's house but got no answer when he rang the bell. So he looked for him at the next most likely place – the Goose's Neck. It was a proper, greasy old pub.

Sure enough, Simp was there, sitting at his favourite table next to the window, the one with the bulging red leather seats. His table was a chaos of interlinking beer rings, as if the Olympics symbol had metastasized.

As soon as the old man caught sight of Mark, he raised a flat palm in greeting. "Mark, son. How goes it? How did the, erm, medicine take – for you and your mum?"

"Not great. I'd rather not talk about that."

"I'm sorry to hear that. You know I can't be serving you here, though, if you catch me drift."

He winked. "I mean, the bar staff are pretty tolerant, but I've already been given a warning and..."

"I've not come for that either."

Mark sat down opposite him. The table above his head was an old marine oil painting. Sedimentary layers of chipped frame, shedding polish like dandruff.

"Alright, lad. I can tell you're stressed. You come and tell your uncle Simp all about it."

"It's not gonna help if you go all Santa Stoner on me. Look, I want to know about Robert Miles, Simp. About how he died."

Simp put his pint down; wiped the yellow sleeve of his shirt across his mouth. "Boy, that's less a blast from the past, and more some buried WW2 munitions. Probably won't go off, but why risk it?"

"Too late. I went to the library to read up about it."

Simp let his head fall back. "The library, eh? You're not the tearaway you used to be, Mark."

"Don't change the subject. Do you know if he had a friend called Craig?"

Simp raised his hands and grinned. "I mean, yeah, probably. Pretty much everyone alive in the 70s had a mate called Craig."

Mark lowered his head and exhaled. Simp was right. This was a stupid line of questioning.

"I'm sorry, lad," Simp added. "I didn't know him all that well and I didn't see him much before he died. Only odd thing I remember is him complaining about this odd sound in his ears. Like a little ditty he couldn't get out of his head. He hummed it to me – must have been something on the radio. It was making him feel quite ill, though."

Mark bit his bottom lip. "Okay, but there was something strange about his body when he was found, wasn't there?"

Simp sighed. "Alright, yes. I didn't see it myself. A drinking buddy did, though. He was a cop, would you believe it?" The old man chortled and shook his head. "Anyway, he'd just joined the force at the time. Not the best first corpse to encounter."

"What... because the body was badly decomposed?"

Simp frowned. "It wasn't so much that..." He breathed out slowly through his nose. "Look, shouldn't you be at your Ma's side right now?"

"She's with a friend. And I don't think she's aware of much now anyway."

"Well, alright then." Simp crossed his arms. "This mate of mine had seen plenty of grisly stuff... suicides pulled out of rivers, old people who ended up dying alone in their houses and nobody realised until the milk started piling up outside. Ghastly, you know, the smell and all, the indignity of it. But when there's bits missing because of animals coming to scavenge and all... well, what's left is all raggedy. The thing with Rob Miles, the holes in his corpse were... My mate said he'd never forget it, not as long as he still drew breath." The old man made the shape of a bowl with his two hands. "Perfectly smooth, like ice cream after someone's dug a scoop into it."

SEVENTEEN

Mark hunched into the collar of his down coat, bag slapping against his thigh. Inside was a photocopied map of the paths in Thurstrop Wood, some pencils and a ruler.

Once he'd gone down the alley, he took out the map. One of the desire paths was veering off crazily from the main path; he sketched it out roughly in florescent pink as he walked.

The paths were muddier than he anticipated. He'd forgotten to put his walking boots on, so the freezing water from the puddles soon seeped into his trainers.

Quite why he was using his two precious hours of freedom to do this, he wasn't sure. But there was something he was trying to see.

The taller tree canopies were a black tangle of varicose veins against the darkening grey of the sky. A powdery, loose snow was on the ground, with that satisfying give that squeaks underfoot. But it had grown dark faster than he'd anticipated. The logs he'd generally navigate by were now hostile white shoulders, indistinguishable from one another.

He shuddered when he first saw the glimmer of the

wire fence around the scrapyard. He wanted to avoid it, obviously. But all the paths seemed to lead there.

His unease grew. Eventually, he stopped drawing and let himself back on one of the trunks.

This was just unbelievable.

He checked the map one last time, to make sure he wasn't imagining it. But no, it was clear. The photocopy showed a grid of paths. But all the desire paths were wobbly lines heading to one place: the scrapyard.

He needed to get out of the wood. Fucking *now*.

EIGHTEEN

He wasn't quite sure what to do with himself once he got back home.

Helen had arranged for the local vicar to visit Mum. So there the old man was now, sitting by her bedside, giving spiritual advice she probably couldn't hear any longer.

Mark certainly didn't want to think any more about Thurstrop wood or do any more research about Rob Miles or Craig O'Grady. So he cranked up his laptop and started working on the insect track instead.

He added a few layers of sound – a soft thump, like flour bags on an upper floor; a couple of subtle vocalisations. But after some tweaking, he got bored and decided to try something different.

He hadn't yet used the new speakers Helen had bought him. They were kind of retro, with big black cones, covered by nylon. Idly, he took some bicarb of soda from the kitchen and sprinkled it over them. Then, connecting up the speakers to his laptop, he began to play the track.

He wasn't really expecting much – maybe concentric circles, like the kind you got when you dropped a pebble into calm water. But what appeared on the speakers made him blink and hold his breath.

The powder formed ridges, lines flowing sinuously around each other like a labyrinth. And they were familiar.

He turned off the track. Hands shaking, he took out the makeshift map from Thurstrop Wood. There was no need to compare side by side – the sketch he'd made of the paths and the powder pattern were a very clear match.

———

HE WAS ON BEXTON LANE, about halfway to Thurstrop Wood, when a car alarm behind him went off. He could have sworn he hadn't touched the thing at all. But what stopped him in his tracks was the rhythm of the horn.

Little bit of hash, a hand job and some POOOOOOOOOO-PPERS

All he could do for a moment was stare at the car, dumbstruck. He was standing there long enough for the owner, a tall balding guy, to come out and of his house and switch off the alarm with his key fob.

The man directed a hostile stare at Mark. "What is it?" he demanded. "Did you set it off?"

But Mark didn't answer. Now that the alarm had gone quiet, the feeder pillar just a little further up the street was buzzing. Same rhythm. *Little bit of hash, a hand job and some* POOOOOOOOOO-PPERS

The car owner rolled his eyes. "Have to call someone out to deal with that. Kid, you seem a bit dazed. Are you lost?" Mark said nothing.

Exactly how freely was he walking back up to Thurstrop Wood? He couldn't even remember making the decision to leave the house.

Fuck it.

He continued walking.

"Weirdo…," the guy muttered behind him.

Back in the wood, he felt briefly safe and enclosed, listening to the wind. There was an odd, growling-stomach comfort to it.

But then the call came. *Little bit of hash, a hand job and some POOOOOOOOOO-PPERS*. This time it sounded like it might be coming from an owl.

Again, not feeling entirely in control of his own feet, Mark tried to move in the direction of the sound. Dread surged in him as he veered towards the scrapyard.

But the owl's call was fainter – it wasn't coming from there. He turned left, along one of the weirdly divergent desire paths.

The call, again. But now it didn't sound like it was coming from a bird, but instead some kind of electronic device.

It had become colder very fast. The leaves under his feet were partly frozen; they made one hell of a crunch, like the sound of ccreal being eaten on an advert.

He came to a small clearing, not one he recognised. It was one of those dips in the ground that might have been where a Luftwaffe shell had dropped. More likely it was just a sink hole – the sort of spot he might have gone to for some BMX-ing 8 years ago.

Now he could *see* where the call was coming from.

A single bare tree, with low hanging branches, was growing from the bottom of the dusty dip. Perched amongst its branches were dozens and dozens of old appliances: fire alarms, landline phones and fax machines, other things whose use Mark didn't even know.

Like some kind of weird chorus, they were all bleeping to that same rhythm.

What was this? Some kind of fucking shrine?

He started to jog down the slope towards them, and they stopped. All at once.

He was freaked out enough to want to clamber back up, but the slope was too steep and he almost tumbled down, steadying himself on the trunk of the tree at the bottom. When he took his hand away, he realised there was a plaque nailed to the tree. It was wooden, apparently homespun, but the words were clearly machine-carved, in a professional looking font.

THE MUSEUM OF SONIC DEATH.

THE MUSEUM'S *founder started collecting this assemblage of domestic appliances in 1974. They picked up machines whose dying batteries caused them to start beeping. Sometimes the sound is shrill and fast. Other times, it's an infrequent, plaintive cry. It is unknown why the founder created the museum, although rumour has it they were inspired by a nightingale which called hopelessly for a mate in this wood for years, before his song fell silent for good.*

THE SYMPHONY *of these machines is an ever-changing one, enhanced by each new electronic voice added. It is perhaps at its most poignant at dawn. It will close when the final device croaks out its last lament, whether there are human ears to hear it or not.*

·   ·   ·

MARK SHUDDERED. Was this Aurora's work? The plaque looked old enough for that to be a possibility. But surely the forestry officers would have cleared it up long before now?

Not only had all the devices stopped bleeping, there was no sound whatsoever. No birdsong, not even any rustling of wind in the branches. Complete silence thrummed around him – the kind there shouldn't be in a wood or any natural place.

Then, suddenly, the rhythm again. But this time, it wasn't all the devices – just one of them, an old wireless radio wedged in between two small branches. Mark reached out to pull it free. As soon as he did, the noise stopped.

Then came a blast of sound so loud, he almost dropped the radio.

"Mark," a voice sputtered out from inside it. "Is that you?"

Mark froze, his front teeth coming down on his lower lip hard enough to draw blood.

Part of him wanted to run out of the dip, go back home. The voice was weirdly distorted and muffled, as if it was overlaid with another sound and slowed down, but he knew who it was.

"Dad?" His tongue was dry.

More crackling.

"Nothing here but sound, Mark," the voice said. "We drown in her music. She makes us sing and sing and sing. If we still had throats, they would be raw."

A pause. "I have been calling to you, Mark. So much danger."

"Where are you?" Mark asked.

"Not dead." His dad's voice lowered to an anguished growl. "What I'd give for that. Aurora has a token of me."

"Just let me know where you are." Mark hugged the radio close to his stomach, tears stinging his eyes. "I'll get you out of there. I promise."

"No no no, too late. I went far away. I thought if I went far enough, she wouldn't be able to reach me, but she found me. At least she couldn't get you. I took pills to clear my mind, but I couldn't stop my thoughts from straying to Marina, even as my lungs oh god they were like crumpled plastic bags and they wouldn't inflate, but she was there in my mind that first time we kissed I know it must have seemed to you as if there was no love lost between us but at the beginning... I'm just so sor-"

The crackling stopped.

"Dad. No. Come back." Snot and tears were running down Mark's face in rivulets now. "I don't understand. Please."

But the radio was silent. Mark smashed it against the trunk in a fury; stamped on the wires and speakers, sobs ripping from his throat.

The normal sounds of the wood resumed, wind rushing in the trees above him. and now a delicate patter of rainfall.

He wasn't even quite sure what he was crying about. For his dad? For himself? He let the sobs rack him for a while, hugging himself and rocking back and forth. Then he heard that call again – from a bird, somewhere in the direction of the scrap yard.

If he couldn't ask his dad, there was only one other person to go to. If *person* was even the right word for her now.

NINETEEN

His eyes scanned the insect sculptures in the scrapyard warily. But they were all frozen in exactly the same positions they'd been in before.

He walked, unsteadily, up to the sundial.

The scene in the reflection wasn't the same as the one he was standing in. The sculptures were in the same place, but the scrapyard was far tidier, the sheds intact and no weeds to be seen on the ground. The weather was different too: the sort of warm sunlight you get in late autumn, bouncing off the backs of the insect sculptures in blinding sparks.

From the side of the frame, a figure walked into view. Mark's breath caught in his throat.

There was no mistaking those huge dark eyes. Aurora wore a crumpled linen top of light blue, the sun shining through its long trailing sleeves. Her black hair lay in two plaits, slung cavalierly over her shoulders, leaving the collar bone exposed.

She turned to look at Mark and smiled.

Mark's knees went weak. She stepped out of the sundial

as though it were nothing more than a sheet of flowing water. Her chin was slightly lifted, her arms raised. She looked like she was enjoying the ripple and resistance of a light sea breeze.

She had a joint in one hand, which she took a drag on.

"You evil fucking bitch," he whispered.

The words drifted in the air between them like the fumes from her lips.

She laughed and took another drag, before tossing the joint into the dust and treading on it. Not in a sexy These Boots Were Made For Walking way, but with determination, like she was deliberately stamping on an insect.

Her smile was unnervingly still as she advanced towards him. Mark wanted to flee, but he was rooted to the ground.

Soon, she was in front of him. He breathed in an odd, delicate tracery of a scent. Something floral?

She raised her arms, draped them round his neck, and rocked from side to side. Then she pinched his chin between her thumb and forefinger.

Her lips yielded quickly as they pressed to his. His hands slid down her back, exposed by a deep dip and a lot of cross laces, then further, to the crescent of her buttocks under her jeans.

With a quick smirk, she pulled away from him, walked towards the abandoned badger sett or whatever it was. She ran a finger along its contours, her eyes still on him.

"Wouldn't it be strange, don't you think, if all the odd swellings here grew larger? If they stretched like balloon rubber, all translucent, and you could see the life beneath. Teeming like cancerous cells metastasizing." He could tell she was looking for a reaction from him; he tried not to give her one.

"Look at that hole there..." She pointed down to a small, cave-like crevice, an ellipse of darkness. "What is that hole pulled tighter – like the mouth of a drawstring purse?"

Still facing him, she leaned back and put both her hands on top of the highest mound of the sett, and looked back round at him, her eyes a challenge.

He approached her, and she put her arms round his neck. He pressed himself up against her, ran a hand over her breasts. She let out a long sigh, then started to loosen her belt.

"What are you doing?" he whispered.

She lifted up her fingers, and closed his eyelids. "Hush now."

All he could hear was the birdsong: the rich tapestry of sound you only got in early spring.

Little bit of hash, a hand job and some POOOOOOOOOO-PPERS...

Dad's song.

It yanked him out of his trance.

He seized her shirt and flung her away from the mound. "Get the fuck away from me."

She laughed as she regained her balance. "Fucking. Yes. You were pretty keen on that last time I saw you. Is it only boys, though?"

"Boys and girls. But definitely not demons."

"Oh darling..." Aurora took one of her plaits and played with the tuft of dark hair at the end, shaking her head. "It would be a lot better for you if I were as straightforward a thing as a demon."

"What are you, then?"

"My kind has many names. I am unusual, in that I started out as a human being. Most of the others are dullard spirits, content to keep the dead in their hives until they're ripe for what comes next. But I keep mine for harvest. I have a little token of them all, from just before their spark was extinguished. Because I have not abandoned my physical form, as you should know having just touched me. I am flesh still, and I need feeding."

"You keep people's souls in this wood?"

She nodded. "Thurstrop Wood is a sebaceous cyst of this world, the life force of the dear ones building up in my pustule."

"Until it bursts?" Mark stooped to pick up a stone, and held it over the mound.

A shadow of alarm passed over her face. But then she laughed. "Oh, darling. Do you think I've got them all stored in there? They can't be held in that way, by a physical barrier. They're trapped in the sounds of this wood, just like your Daddy. Or sometimes the smells, depending on temperament. I think your mother might be a smell, somehow. You, on the other hand, you're definitely a texture – maybe that particularly smooth feeling of a young silver birch trunk..."

She walked up to him again and reached towards his face. He slapped her hand away.

"You have my mother, then."

"I will do soon. She was the last living being in the thoughts of your father."

"... And Dad the last person Craig saw before he fell from the crane. He caught it from him, didn't he?"

"Caught it?" Aurora smiled sweetly. "It's not like a disease, sweetheart. It's an honour – eternal life, so much more exhilarating than what would otherwise be in store. You'll see soon. You're likely be the last person in your mother's thoughts. All these dreams and visions you've been having... it's like Russian dolls. You hold all the most traumatic memories of the others in your trail."

Mark barked out a bitter laugh. "You seem very confident I'd be the last person in my mother's thoughts. You clearly don't know her that well."

"Oh, the last person you think of isn't always one you care the most about. I mean, take Rob, that old goat. Can you believe the last person he was thinking of was his good mate Craig instead of me, in all my splendour?"

"How did you start this?"

Aurora smiled at that. "For many years, I studied the spells and incantations; not just here, but from all over the world. I picked up one book that was only images – abstract and repetitive patterns that did not belong to any culture I had ever come across. I thought, for a long time, it must be an ancient alphabet. But it was, in fact, a score. I won't give it the name of music, because once I learned how to identify the sounds and recreate them – it was nothing as frivolous as what human beings would call song. And I summoned a being of the cosmos you would never be able to comprehend. You couldn't even start to wrap her in your flimsy coat of understanding. She is, I suppose, a goddess, one whose worshippers were wiped out in a cataclysm. They fed her with noise, that music human beings could never create themselves. Even a note would dissolve your paltry physical matter.

She still hungers for the songs and sounds of other planets, although they can never satisfy her. You should all be grateful I stole from her the signal, the one she uses to draw creatures towards her eternal nest. Without it, she is powerless, dormant, and I control her army of workers.

I built these sculptures, you know, as tributes to her. They serve as my new puppets. I know you've seen one of them in action already. Perhaps you'd like to see the others?"

She opened her arms and performed a kind of shimmer with her body, her shoulders rotating. The ant made of old globes stirred, its head rotating towards Mark, its little wire mandibles perking upwards. The beetle's TV aerial antennae quivered as it shifted its aluminium wings. The fly, just a few metres away from him, rose above its log, its Perspex wings a whirring blur – the sound of a hundred cranky office fans. The sun glinted on its legs, which Mark had just enough time to realise were fashioned from tiny, rusting blades, before it swung round towards him.

He turned and ran to the hole in the fence, crouching to get through it. But not quick enough to avoid the scrape of the blades against the back of his neck.

He howled in pain, ripping his trousers away from the brambles as he crawled through the hole. Aurora's giggle followed him as he got to his feet and limped in the direction of the nearest path, the blood trickling its cool way down his back.

TWENTY

By the time he was back home, the last of the snow had finally melted under a heavy deluge. His entire body was a yawning ache. The blood that had run down the back of his neck had crusted over. He was shivering, from terror or cold or both.

Once he was indoors, he laid his hands on one of the radiators just to get some feeling into them.

Mum always said he had no resolve, no determination. But he'd achieved an odd mental clarity once he'd escaped from the scrapyard.

This would be one hell of a way to show her.

He stripped off his muddy trousers, the wind outside howling with operatic abandon. The sound of rain battering the windows was a comforting one, though.

After he'd got dressed and done his best to clean and disinfect the cuts, he went to his mother's bedroom.

Helen was on the other side of the bed. She didn't reproach him; barely even looked up at him. Her voice was hoarse. "The nurse says she's likely in her final hours. She's called the hospice nurses."

Mark took a deep breath. The plan was solidifying.

If he could make Helen leave the bedside, he could focus Mum's attention on him in her last moments.

After she died, he would go to the woods, find that dip again. He'd try to talk to Dad. Failing that, he'd at least make sure his thoughts were on Dad before he set a blade to his wrists or OD'd or whatever. Perhaps they'd be reunited in Aurora's limbo. He didn't see there was much for him to stick around for in this life. He'd never been suicidal, but then, he'd never really had any passions or ambitions either. Who would really miss him now?

Perhaps Helen, for a little bit, but he was pretty sure that was only because he'd be the final remnant of his mother.

She lowered her head.

He noticed she did not have that familiar slash of green above her eyes today; just heavy bags beneath. It was the first time he'd seen her entirely without make-up. He found himself focusing on a mole on the left of her nose, one he'd never seen before. How could he have been looking at someone for all those years and not notice something like that?

The doorbell played its Debussy, and Helen got up, wiping her eyes, to let the nurses in. Mark followed her.

The nurses were disconcertingly jolly and matter of fact, pulling out their PPE and scrubbing up in the kitchen.

One of them got the syringe ready. The other connected Mum up to an ECG and blood pressure monitor. "Just so you can see how things are going."

"I think we've pretty much done as much as we can to make her comfortable now," one nurse told him. "Just ring if you feel you need help. It might be quite a few hours." She patted Mark's shoulder. Before they left, she handed him a card with her number on it.

When he came back from leading them outside, Mum's breathing was a weird, deflated snore. He was, quite suddenly, shocked by her loss of weight. The night dress was hanging off her. Her yellowed skin had a distinct grey tinge to it now.

He got up, stood at the window and massaged his temples. How could he get Helen to leave?

"Don't you want to come and sit with her?" she asked him plaintively.

"No." His answer was abrupt. Pretty much the only way to go about this was with brutality.

"Mark, this is the last time we can sit with her, talk to her."

"Yeah, and thank God for that."

"That's a terrible thing to say." Her voice caught in her throat.

"True one, though. I think you got the best of her. In fact, I know it. I've read it in your own words."

Helen became very still. Her hands in her lap clenched.

Mark chuckled. "Relax, I'm in awe. I've got to give it to you both, I'd never have guessed."

"You found the letters I wrote, then."

"Yeah. Under the bed."

She crossed her arms, averted her eyes. "You must have had a good long read."

"No, just one of them. You'd had an argument."

Her hands folded themselves into a tight little knot. She breathed out through her nose. "We didn't have many causes to row."

"What kind of things did you argue about?"

She shrugged. "You, mostly."

"Of course. What *about* me, just out of interest?"

"One of your visits to the police station about a year ago, after your latest adventures on drugs. Marina had decided she'd had enough. She thought it would be best for you to leave home, thought it might get you to grow up and take responsibility for yourself."

He snorted. "She was worried school might find out, you mean. Oh, and I bet you'd have liked the house just to yourselves..."

Helen stared at him hard, folding her arms. "Well, actually, Mark, that was what the argument was about. I thought she should give you another chance. And she did, ultimately."

"Thanks... I guess."

"She loved you, Mark. Loves you." She leaned over and stroked Mum's hair with a forefinger. The tears were falling again now. "I know she didn't show it in a way you recognised..."

"She couldn't bear the sight of me. And I always thought it was because she could see Dad in me. But it wasn't that, was it? She could see a whole load of *herself* in me."

Helen frowned for a moment, then her gaze dropped as realisation struck. "Oh. Oh, I see."

"Yeah."

This was quite a way to come out to someone for the first time. Mark could almost have laughed.

She breathed in deeply and closed her eyes. "It wasn't that she was ashamed of who she... of who *we* are. It was just... she didn't much like the culture around all that." Helen grimaced.

"Embarrassed by the leather boys and the furries, is it?"

"I know it's hard for people of your age to understand.

Marina and I were of a very different time. I can remember boys when I was your age, making obscene scissoring gestures with their hands, sticking notes on people's backs – "lesbo," and so on. Marina always preferred the term "sapphic.'"

"Right. So it would all have been okay if I'd framed it as an ancient Greek, high culture thing? Perhaps I should have painted myself orange like one of those dudes on the vases and thrown a discus..."

Helen scraped her chair against the floor, her eyes still closed. "You're angry, and no doubt you have your reasons. But I need some quiet now. I'm going to pray for her."

"I think you should leave. Right fucking now. You can pray somewhere else."

Helen shook her head. "I deserve to be here as much as you do, Mark. You know that."

She lowered herself to her knees beside the bed, taking his mother's hands, her lips moving slightly.

"Helen, I'm ordering you to go. I'm her son and I don't want you here."

He was doing his best to sound angry, resolute. But it came out wheedling and desperate.

Again, she shook her head. "I'm sorry, Mark." It was a long sorry: a sheet wafting over a bed it wouldn't quite be able to cover.

Mum's breathing had changed to a sort of obstructed gurgle. There wasn't much time left.

One thing was becoming clear. There was no way he was going to be able to keep Helen from his mother's bedside, unless he dragged her out of there.

He went to the downstairs bathroom and opened the medicine cabinet. After a quick rummage round the top shelf, he detected the presence of a plastic sachet. He'd been right: there was still a stash of Simp's pills in there, that he had forgotten about until just now. He reached for the sachet and tipped a pill out. It rested at the confluence of the lines in his palm.

He went back to the kitchen and made a cup of tea, ensuring it was the well-done toast colour Helen liked, with a full spoon of sugar – that would, he hoped, disguise the flavour of the pill. He stirred it with the teaspoon, and it dissolved quickly.

Taking it into the bedroom, he offered it to her as casually as he could. "I'm sorry. I shouldn't have said those things to you."

She looked up, her eyes red. She took the cup from him; had one sip and grimaced. Mark held his breath, waiting.

And then, obligingly, she tipped back the whole lot.

"Thank you," she gasped. "I didn't realise how much I needed that."

For a while, she continued to kneel by the bed, holding mum's hand. Until her eyes grew heavy, and her head began to droop.

Mark was at her side quickly. "Helen – are you okay? You're very pale." He helped her up, guided her to the armchair near the window. "I think you might faint... Look, why don't you sit there, try and get some sleep?"

"I can't. I can't go to sleep with your mother like this." But her voice was already faint and woozy.

"Don't worry. I'll stay awake, tell you if anything changes."

He waited a good long time, until she was breathing very deeply, before he covered her with a blanket and turned the chair away from his mother's bed.

He exhaled. Hopefully, that would do it.

TWENTY-ONE

Mum had been positioned on her side by the nurses, propped up by heavy pillows, presumably to avoid pressure on the tumour. Even through the flannel of her nightie, Mark could make out the familiar round lump at the base of her back.

He kneeled next to her and applied a slight pressure to the inside of her palm. Her eyes, pinkish and gummy at the lids, opened a little.

She was whispering something. He lowered his head to her dried-out lips. After a couple of attempts, he managed to make out what she was saying. "Helen..."

"I'm sorry, Mum. She can't be here." *Shit.*

He had to get her mind focused on him. He started talking, rapidly, trying to keep his voice low and soothing.

"Mum – do you know the snow has gone now? Remember the heavy snowfall when I was little, you'd always be out there with me, with the sleigh? And that time I wanted to have a carrot nose and big coal buttons, but you didn't have those, so we used three black velvet pin cushions?"

This was all true. Whenever they got a fall, she'd always be out there with him, making snow angels and having snowball fights. That was pretty much the only time he could remember her smiling at him, genuinely.

She was making a monumental effort to speak now, screwing her eyes up in pain.

He again leaned down, so his ear was close to her mouth. "Going... to be taken. See my back."

Taken? Did she have some kind of awareness of what was happening to her? He'd been under the impression she'd been blotto the last few weeks.

His heart hammered as he walked to the other side of the bed.

"Fucking hell." Blood was soaking through her nightie, around the tumour. Quickly, he undid the buttons, his fingers trembling.

The skin of her back was straining, cracking like an egg being tapped from the inside, the little pulses regular. He grabbed some of the towels at her bedside. Just as he was about to apply pressure to her back, Mum managed to twist her head round towards him. She caught his gaze and held it, eyes wide.

"Get... out."

He staggered back a few paces.

She was still lying on her side. But the skin around the tumour had peeled away, blood seeping in a huge arc round the back of the nightgown. Rising from her torn flesh were insect legs, about the length of a forearm, waving frantically in the air. They weren't black but a peculiarly translucent white, each one like a couple of very thin cable wires twisted around each other.

As the air forced itself from his lungs, Mark realised he was looking at nerves.

He walked slowly back towards her, his heart pounding. He caught a brief glimpse of

the underside of the thing extracting itself from his mother, the motion accompanied by an awful, sucking pluck, like a thumb being pulled from a resisting mouth.

Head, thorax, abdomen. Each body part eased itself out of the gaping wound. The huge ant that emerged wasn't black, but the deep pink of a small intestine.

It dropped out of his mother and tumbled to the floor.

It was about the size of a rugby ball, entirely made of guts and gristle, apart from its wings, which were the queasy phlegm-yellow of old fingernail clippings. Before Mark had a chance to react, it lifted them and flew in a whirring zigzag out of the door.

Where the lump in his mother's back had been was now a perfect bowl of scooped out flesh. A notch of severed vertebra protruded from the gore and the deep purplish brown of the liver, obscenely like a little beckoning finger.

His mother's body convulsed as the blood flowed from her wound, thick and sluggish. He made a lunge for her; cupped her face in his hands. He needed to get her focus on him.

"Look at me, Mum."

She opened her mouth, and although there was no sound, he could make out what she was saying. "Helen..."

A blast of buzzing from behind startled him, and he turned round. Helen was still sleeping but her finger was on the buzzer, tapping out a rhythm.

Little bit of hash, a hand job and some POOOOOOOOOOO-PPERS...

Mark forced himself up with a roar and whacked the monitor out from under her finger. Helen woke up, blinking rapidly.

"Mark, what's going on?" she demanded, her voice weak. Then her eyes settled on his mother.

"You little bastard, what have you done to her?"

She tumbled out of her chair. Helen wasn't a large woman, but she immediately backed him towards the door.

"Helen, no, you've got to get away from Mum, you..."

She silenced him with a punch to the diaphragm, which sent him reeling backwards instantly."

Nausea rose, and he could feel the vomit's acid touch at the back of his throat. He moaned.

Helen kneeled by his mother and took her hand. Mum's eyes, filled with those final tears of death, settled on her.

A slow exhalation escaped Mum's lips as the ECG monitor retreated to a steady, flat hum.

TWENTY-TWO

From the alleyway, Mark's usual path into Thurstrop Wood was like the pupil of an eye, surrounded by a hazel-green iris.

He had no recollection of how he'd got there.

The pain in his chest, where he was pretty sure Helen had broken a rib, pulsated with a warmth not unlike the desire he'd last felt for Tom.

Sirens tore into the air, somewhere quite nearby. Perhaps Helen had already called the police. He'd better hurry up.

As he walked into the wood, an odd calm fell over him. The birdsong seemed flatter, more soothing than usual – far more cooing and warbling than the rasping calls of jays and crows. A crackling fire of noise, welcoming and seductive.

This was what Simp would call a good trip, in that it felt as though someone else was taking the reins of his mind, guiding him along on a nice gentle ride. His fear was gone now; he knew what to do. Clenching his hand a little tighter around his mobile phone, he carried on walking.

There were still dots of snow and ice around, nestled in

crevices of logs and balanced precariously on branches, pristine white smears. But Mark took one of the desire paths and walked down it at a steady pace.

When he got to the scrapyard, part of the fence had been torn down. He walked over what remained of it.

The sundial with its grasshopper pointer glinted in the sun. He stood directly opposite it. And there, where his reflection should have been, was Aurora. She wore not the same clothes as before, but a long baggy clown suit with a pom-pom on the tip of each breast, and beautiful harlequin eye make-up in slashes of purple and silver – what must have been the costume she used for her shows.

She was holding the ant formed of his mother's viscera, tickling its abdomen as if it was a kitten.

He walked right up to the mirror. From under the large stain of blue around her lips.

she bestowed on him a bland, benign smile.

"Commiserations, Mark."

She lifted the ant up to her ear, so its head brushed her cheeks. "How do you like it?" she asked him.

Mark's throat went dry. "How do I like what?"

"Well, your mother's new form, I suppose. She will be one of my workers, before she becomes a sound or smell or texture. This is a sort of... pupal stage. When it first extracts itself, a soul has more grist to it than you'd think. It's not the airy, insubstantial thing that so many medieval philosophers took it for it for." She waggled her fingers and laughed, before touching the ant's head with her lips. "This one is a fresh darling, so the memories are raw. It's strange, you know. What they remember. Anyway, you were right about your mother." She put the ant down to scuttle over her feet. "She made sure it was Helen who was the last person in her thoughts. She wanted what remained of her mind to be free of you. A truly putrid disappointment of a son – couldn't excel at school and didn't even manage to be much of a tearaway, either. I wonder what I'll make of your soul? It's malleable, so I feel it would best be rendered a texture. Perhaps the texture of clay about to be fired in the kiln. Because there's plenty of wetness in you. You're not quite *done*, are you? But there's just a hint of grit as well. And an artist shouldn't complain about their materials. You'll do."

Mark turned away from her without a word and headed towards the mound.

"Oh, sweetheart," she called after him. "Are you still thinking you can break that mound apart and that will be an end to my collection?"

"No. But something else might be."

He began to tap at his mobile phone, swiping quickly through his tracks until he got to the one he wanted.

Phengaris Blues

His finger lingered for a moment over Play.

"What are you doing?" Aurora's voice was still as roundly assured as a swill of hot chocolate on the palate. Yet there was just a touch less amusement in it than there had been.

Mark turned for a moment and smiled. "I think I've got something for you that might jog a few memories."

He pressed Play, and out blared the track. It was as clear as bird song in the silence of the scrapyard.

"Where in hell did you get that?" There was a raw, serrated edge of panic in her voice now. He pressed Pause, still smiling at her.

"From a conversation you had with a journalist a long, long time ago. And he wasn't as honest with you as you thought. When I first heard it, I thought it might make for a nice song. But it's a hell of a lot more than a song, isn't it? It's a signal, one you've been jamming with another one for a long time now."

He put a hand on the mound. It was oddly warm to the touch, as if it had been baking in sunlight for hours, rather than under a recent layer of frost.

Mark began to tap out that rhythm, singing as he did so. "*Little bit of hash, a hand job and some* POOOOOOOOOO-*PPERS...*"

Aurora banged on the mirror with her fists. For some reason, it wasn't giving way to her as it had done before.

"Let's see what happens when we play this track of ours instead," he said. "I've called it *Phengaris Blues*. Do you know about the Phengaris Blue, Aurora? It's a little butterfly that can pretend to be an ant queen by sending out the right sounds and smells. The workers do her bidding. But if that signal doesn't work any longer, what do you reckon the workers do to her? Shall we find out?"

He put his mobile next to the mound and pressed Play. Beneath his fingers, it started to vibrate.

"Stop!" Aurora's scream filled the scrapyard. "If you stop, I'll release your parents. I will let them die, I promise. Please, stop. You don't understand."

Under his trainers, Mark could feel the same vibrations. Pure exhilaration filled him. He wasn't sure he *could* stop now, even if he wanted to.

He turned back to look at the sun dial.

Aurora still had his mother's flesh ant in her arms, clutching it to her abdomen. But the gentle autumn light behind the mirror had turned to a sullen, orange glow. Her long hair was being blown forwards as if by a wind. Between the dark strands, he could still make out the eyes. He was expecting hatred, but what he saw instead was a terrible awe. She was looking not at him, but *past* him.

"Oh, she is hungry," Aurora said, voice hoarse. "Can you not feel that hunger? No hymns on this earth, the bird-song, none of its weak human pleas will be able to satiate her." Aurora's laughter came again, shot through with the wild cadences of madness. "She has heard her song, and it fills the great chambers of her memory. She will be Queen again."

Something moved under Mark's fingers. He yelped and dropped the mobile phone. The top of the mound was cracking, he saw – giving way to rivulets of ants, all with their tiny green spots. They streamed towards the sundial.

And covered it.

Then the flesh ants in the mirror world were crawling over Aurora, wrenching her throat apart, the sides of her face pinched together like the hole of a button. The painted patches of blue around her mouth and eyes caved in, leaving dark, gaping holes in their place.

With another blast from behind, the numerals etched into the surface of the mirror began to shift – coming apart and crossing over one another haphazardly. The mirror shattered along its lines.

A moment of heavy silence followed – that same odd silence Mark had noticed when he was talking to his dad.

For a few moments, he could only breathe.

A flesh ant scuttled past him.

The mound was nothing more than a gaping wound in the earth now. But something was rising from it. He could make out the shape of the thorax and abdomen, as tall as a tree, and – oh, oh fuck, the *wings*.

They quivered and spread, so completely covered in ants that they were a solid expanse of darkness, the dots of the green coalescing into great veins.

He opened his mouth, his head and his throat vibrating

with a scream. But he could hear nothing. The sound had been torn from him, drawn towards the rearing vortex before him. And his breath was teased out after it.

He dropped to his knees, then fell forwards. His mouth opened and closed as he spasmed on the ground. But there was no oxygen any longer for him to gulp down. Before he lost consciousness, he caught a glimpse of the sky between the tree canopies – the sort of blue you'd normally see in late September, when the light had the quality of sherry in a glass, and would settle on the rooftops in a brief, dazzling glimmer before the sun sank out of view.

TWENTY-THREE

She expanded over the twitching scrap of life before her, inhaling the scent of death. At that initial stage, it was a subtle delight. A cirrus wisp; not the cumulo nimbus of rot and decay.

Her twisting labyrinth of ears had once received tribute in the form of songs, at frequencies that could never be replicated on Earth. The sacrifice of this petty being was barely a ripple across an ocean that yearned for the great pull of tides. She needed noise with the power of gravitational waves.

His final scream was the Goddess's second taste of the sonic-food of this world.

And it was so very far from satisfying.

ACKNOWLEDGMENTS

Phengaris came out in an untidy rush, after a very strange experience in a familiar wood near my house, just after Christmas. I kept the drafts to myself for quite a while, partly because I really wasn't sure where I was going with it for a long time. But there were, as always, plenty of people who I owe thanks to for getting it to publication stage. They include:

Nat and Shauna of Nefarious Bat Press, for their astute editing and warm welcome to the world of long form publishing. It has been an absolute pleasure.

Ruth Anna Evans, for the enigmatic and gorgeous cover design.

Bob Fear, Shantell Powell and Jennifer Cornick for all the sensitive and sympathetic critiques over a year of workshops. Jennifer will be able to trace the marks of her able beta reading in the novella.

Alex Davis, whose feedback on an early draft of this novella gave me the courage to finish and submit it.

Lydia Massiah, Lorna Riley, Sally Doherty, Marisa Blagden and Caroline Murphy, for plenty of encouragement and prodding over the dry periods. I never did manage to get anything I wrote for kids over the line, but I don't regret the years spent chatting.

My husband Gareth and children Owain and Ellie, for putting up with me tearing my hair out in front of a screen for so long.

And finally my mother, who always believed I could do it and let me read a lot of very dark literature at an impressionable age.

ABOUT THE AUTHOR

Anna Orridge lives in London with her family and works for an environmental charity. Her short fiction has appeared in Mslexia, the Gothic Nature Journal and the anthologies 'Rock Band' and 'Rewired', published by Ghost Orchid Press. Her essay, *Bihexuality in The Craft* is published in the Off Limits Press anthology 'Divergent Terror'. She has a great fondness for corvids and tardigrades.

ABOUT NEFARIOUS BAT PRESS

Nefarious Bat Press is a women-owned independent publisher specialising in queer and inclusive, intersectional feminist horror, crime and dark fiction.

Find them online at www.nefariousbatpress.com

www.ingramcontent.com/pod-product-compliance
Lightning Source LLC
Chambersburg PA
CBHW071005120726
47910CB00004B/1387